Trouble Down South and Other Stories

by

Katrina Parker Williams

(A Storyteller of Tales)

DEDICATION

Dedicated to my husband, Stephon, and my mother, Rachel, to my second parents, Aunt Clara, Frances, and Eddie, and to all of my brothers and sisters. Thank you all for being a wonderful support system for me. To all of my good friends and close family (you all know who you are), thank you for keeping me grounded.

CONTENTS

Katrina Parker Williams

REVOLT IN THE CHEROKEE NATION

Revolts they fear, not the slave masters who reigned in the Antebellum South but a new oppressor, the Five Civilized Tribes, forced themselves from their own homelands.

The Cherokees, Choctaws, and Chickasaws, Creeks, Seminoles, and brethren of mixed blood; they are the offspring of white settlers intermarrying into the tribes, and they are the chief slaveholders.

The Mixed-bloods depend on their Black brethren for unpaid labor in the parched fields; full-blooded Indians rely on them also as English interpreters and translators.

Indian slaveholders, some callous and pitiless, treat their chattel with inhumanity; the English hire them to seek runaway slaves, a lucrative enterprise they enjoy.

1

Indian slaveholders, some kind and generous, refuse to return runaway slaves they capture; they welcome them as family into their tribes, a shared bond they both benefit from.

The Seminoles are of a different breed, however, never engaging in chattel slavery; they take in fugitive slaves as their own property, the runaways seeking solace amongst them.

Fear surfaces amongst four of the Civilized Tribes; a fear of revolt, a threat of uprisings prevail. The tribes establish slave codes to squelch insurrections; all but the Seminoles are willing to comply.

The Seminoles' slaves are allowed to roam freely, carrying weapons, owning livestock and horses, possessing land and property like freed men, posing great threats to the security of the Cherokees.

The slaves plan their escape as early morning dawns, before the Cherokees rise and know their fate; they lock in their masters and overseers while they repose in slumbered ignorance.

They burglarize Joseph Vann's provisions store, taking guns and horses too, mules, ammunition, and food they plunder for their secretive passage to freedom.

Men, women, and children make away and rendezvous at the appointed meeting place, journeying toward Mexico to seek refuge in a free country where slavery is prohibited.

The freedom seekers take flight; through the Creek Nation they travel; other enslaved brethren join suit, undiscovered until daylight appears.

Their escape, when discovered, prompt their Cherokee masters to take pursuit, following the escapees into the Creek Nation; the Cherokee and Creek join forces for faster detection.

Continuing on into the Choctaw Nation, a battle ensues; the fugitive runaways prepare for combat against their pursuers, both sides suffering loss and casualties; for two days no victor is proclaimed.

Unprepared for the resistance from the runaways, the Cherokees and Creeks seek reinforcements; they retreat, leaving the fugitives to continue on toward the Red River, their immediate destination.

Carrying eight runaways from the Choctaw Nation, two patty rollers meet with a deadly fate; the Cherokee and Creek fugitives set free the procured eight who join with them en route to Mexico.

The Cherokee National Council establishes a militia, led by John Drew, to hunt the runaways; they accost the fugitives short of the Red River.

The fugitive slaves offer no resistance; starving, cold, and disillusioned they are. Five arrested for murder, and all but two captured, they are returned to their Cherokee slave owners.

SLAVE AUCTION

Horatio woke up next to his mother on a pallet atop planks laid across puncheons that were fitted in holes bored into the walls. It was not yet daybreak, and he was wide awake. He lay there for a moment and then looked up at his mother who was lying on a pallet across from him staring out the window.

Less than two weeks earlier, after a lengthy illness Master Paul Finnius had died, leaving behind his elderly wife and two sons. Word spread that the sons wanted to sell off the family estate. An auction had been planned as soon as possible to stave off more heartache for the mistress at having to deal with the business matters of her husband's estate. She was in no position to run the plantation, and the sons, not wanting to manage the plantation and having their own individual lives, made the decision to sell the plantation and all the associated property, including the twenty-two slaves.

Advertisements had been posted all over town, announcing the public sale of Negroes, and particularly the sale of Master Finnius's slaves. Horatio's mother, Clareene, a mulatto, had learned of the sale from a slave who waited on the mistress in the Big House. Just two days earlier, she had visited the slave quarters late one evening and shared with Clareene the bad news, information Clareene chose not to tell Horatio.

As daylight broke and peered through the slats in the small slave quarter, Clareene stirred. She knew it would not be another long day in the cotton fields, but a sad parting day. She got up, knowing she needed to get her son up and fed and ready to go before the overseer, Dan, made his way on horseback to all the cabins, flicking his flexible, rawhide whip, its menacing snap slicing through the air. Fortunately, this morning she and her son were prepared and ready to go. Horatio assumed they were going to head to the fields as they had always done. But the fields were not their destination.

Dan rode up to the cabins on his horse and yelled out to all the inhabitants, "Let's git a goin'," as he had done many mornings before.

Clareene ushered Horatio out the door to an awaiting wagon. She loaded her son quietly into the wagon and stepped up and stood beside him, watching as other slaves from the cabins mounted the wagon. They were aware of their destination, their saddened faces unsettling everyone who looked upon them. Most of the slaves decided to keep the sad news from their children. It would be best they not know their fate until the absolute last moment. If the Lord have His mercy on them, they may be sold as a family unit, something all of the slaves desperately desired deep in their hearts.

It was a warm June morning. Dew had settled on the grass, and a light breeze cooled the air. Clareene stared at the fusion of blues blanketing the sky above them. Her heart sank at thought of how this day would end. Not well at all. As the wagon pulled off, operated by Dan's slave driver, Clareene could hear the rattling of the wheels against the rocky road. Rocking the inhabitants and knocking them erratically against the wooden rails, the less than sturdy contraption was pulled along by two mules disinclined to go any faster than the driver commanded. Their hooves clomping against the hard clay ground, the mules trudged along begrudgingly, heading past the master's house toward town.

Mistress Finnius's house sat atop the sloping landscape overlooking the slave cabins. Clareene could remember only a few occasions when she had seen the mistress, usually from afar and only when she would make her way into town or on Sundays as she headed off to church. Rarely was the mistress seen outside on the grounds, excepting during these occasions. Today she was nowhere to be seen, not that anyone expected her to be present when slaves that had worked on the plantation for most, if not all of their lives, were being carted off to market and would be leaving the only home they had ever known. Forever.

Dan led the coffle on horseback as his driver herded the mules along behind him. Clareene sat stoic, refusing to look at any of the figures huddled together on the wagon. Her young son clung to her, having no comprehension of what was happening to him; however, he knew something was different. They had never ridden on a wagon before just to head to the fields. They always walked. And when they passed the Big House and headed toward town, he knew it not a typical work day.

"Mama, were're we goin'?" Horatio asked curiously.

"Hush, chile," his mother commanded, noticing a slave woman who was trying desperately to console her whimpering child, hungry and obviously tired from having gotten up at the dawn's break.

Dan glanced back periodically, his menacing stare causing the slave woman to clutch her child more fiercely to quiet it. If her child could not be calmed, she would be subject to a lashing until she could comfort it.

The wagon eased into the city of Natchez, Mississippi and headed downtown. Dan led the wagonload of slaves down the center of town to the far end to a large open field next to the horse stables where the auction would take place. The wagon stopped in front of the stables, and the slaves were unloaded and herded to a room inside.

The slaves for sale were held in the horse stables for a day and a half, awaiting the beginning of the auction. Interested buyers visited the stables early to inspect the slaves and determine an appropriate value for the human chattel. People from all over the states made their way to the auction as well as potential buyers from neighboring states. The town was flooded with visitors, quickly appropriating available lodging in preparation for the auction.

On the day of the sale, several male Negroes were dragged out of the stables and led to the auction block. Several gentlemen of means stood to the right of the auction block, away from the frenzy of would-be buyers inspecting the stock of slaves standing ashamedly in a huddle, unclothed, greased, and most obviously distraught. They had fancied several Negroes that would fit their bill and decided what they were willing to bid on them.

At first call for the bidding was a Negro family of five, a well-built father, stocky and tall, and his timid wife whose modesty overtook her, and their three children, a son and two daughters. They did not want to be split up, and he pleaded with the potential buyers trying to induce them to take them as a whole. His pathetic appeals fell on deaf ears, and many of the prospectors were interested only in buying slaves to be resold. It

8

was more difficult to resell a whole family as opposed to an individual Negro.

In the stables, the second group of Negroes was being prepared to be rounded up for the auction. Clareene watched from the stables' entrance as the bidding began. She listened intently to the pleas of the Negro father. If he could be persuasive and convince a buyer to purchase his whole family, she figured there may be hope for her and her son. She knew his happiness depended on keeping her family together. She had lost her husband years earlier to the auction block, and she feared a similar, if not worst, fate for her son. She hoped the prospectors would be sympathetic to the Negro man's pleas, but to her dismay, they were not.

A gentleman from Louisiana bought the Negro man and his son, a fate worse than death for the Negro father. He pleaded earnestly with his new master to purchase his wife and daughters, knowing it futile to appeal to his sense of morality and compassion, but focused instead on divulging the benefit of his worth in flesh and blood. His appeal once again fell on deaf ears. Another man from Georgia purchased his wife and two daughters, the devastated mother clinging desperately to her young son, refusing to part with her first born. Distraught and overcome with grief, the Negro father coerced his sobbing wife to free their son, fearing a lashing from her new owner.

Clareene was Chattel Number 13 in the catalogue, and Horatio, Number 14. When it was time to be examined, they were stripped of their modest clothing down to their bare skin. They were washed in greasy water so that their bronzed skin would glisten in the mid-morning sunlight, making them look sleek and healthy and fit. The cruel, sadistic face of the slaveholder examining them burned into their minds as he chained them together preparing to lead them to the block.

Moments later Chattel No. 13 and 14 from the catalogue were called to the block. Clareene was hauled out in chains first, then her son. She waited with baited breath, hoping they would be sold as a family. They were examined by another male slaveholder as the prospective buyers stood around them, inspecting all of the stock. They walked around Horatio and his mother, staring them up and down and looking for any signs of disfigurement or lameness, just as their master had done to the many horses and cattle he had purchased over the years.

The buyers examined the inside of their mouths and inspected their teeth. One prospective buyer felt Clareene's breasts to determine how fit she'd be to breed more children, Clareene cringing from the humiliation of it all. They observed her limbs for signs of muscular fitness and checked every crack and crevice that could conceal hidden wounds and bruises, something that could surely deter a prospective buyer. They wanted healthy slaves. Bruises, scars, or wounds would indicate a sickly or lame product, something they did not want.

Clareene was bid off first and was made to stand with the other Negros previously purchased by their new owners. Then when her oldest child, her only son, was put on the auction block, she was paralyzed with grief. The buyers had assembled around the block, prepared to bid on her child. She fought back the tears, but she could not fathom having to part forever from her child. She could not bear to see her son reduced to such a fate. Lord only knows the fate some young child slaves face once torn from their mothers' bosoms.

Horatio had caught the attention of several bidders as he stood naked on the auction block. When the bidding began, Clareene tore away from the purchased group of Negroes and pushed her way to the front of the group of buyers, pleading with her new master to purchase her only son. With a look of remonstrance and entreaty, she clung to his ankles, beseeching him in as pitiable a voice as a sinner bargaining with the devil to reconsider and spare her child from a fate worse than death. He looked down at her, perfectly passionless and embittered by her supplication, and struck her across the back of her head with such violent force that she momentarily lost her ability to speak. Then he kicked her in the ribs, knocking her to the side, her body wincing in pain, and then with all the energy she could muster, she crept agonizingly away from him.

11

She exclaimed, "Oh Lawd, save muh baby," reaching upwards toward the auction block to touch her child one last time.

But before she could touch Horatio, another gentleman with a grim businesslike demeanor who had won the bid for her child snatched Horatio down from the block and shoved him over to his group of procured and waiting chattel, shocking the child and inciting him into inconsolable tears. Clareene fell to the ground once again, sobbing incessantly. The rough man pulled her up, unconcerned with the pain he had just inflicted on her, and shoved her back over toward his group of purchased Negroes. She was unable to console herself. This was one of Horatio's earliest recollections of the bitterness and brutality of the sale of human chattel. He was in his fourth year and was forced to part from his mother, forever.

In the moments following the auction, Horatio was led away with the other newly-bought Negroes. This moment was the loneliest he had ever felt in his life. Then, suddenly he remembered the instructions of his mother, to turn to God for strength. He closed his eyes tightly and imagined talking directly with Him, asking Him to assuage the pain he was feeling deep inside. His mother had further instructed him to tell God of all his trials and afflictions, and whatever He told him to do, he was to obey.

He asked Him, "Is dis right, Oh Gawd? Is it right fo' me ta be taken fum muh mama?"

His mother would tell him that when he asked God for an answer, to wait, and it would be revealed to him. After a few minutes, he did not receive an answer. Then he wondered how long he must wait.

After the auction ended and the bills of sale were written, the exodus of newly purchased Negroes, bound in shackles and carrying only bundles of modest clothing provided them by their new masters, marched to the other end of the street to the awaiting steamboats to transport them to their new, unknown destinations.

It had been less than two hours since Horatio was torn from his mother's arms and sold to a buyer from Georgia. He marched his group of Negroes down to the dock to board a steamboat headed to New Orleans. A large group of recently purchased Negroes, tired, distraught, and hungry and chained together in twos, stood in front of his group at the docks waiting to board the steamboat. On the lower deck there was a large compartment where the slaves were to be held, and a strict watch was to be kept over them by other Negro slaves to prevent their escaping when the steamboat docked at the landing ports to load supplies, equipment, and more slaves.

As the steamboat headed out of Natchez, Horatio, frail, hungry, and petrified, sat chained to a young slave boy of fourteen. He had no understanding of what was happening to him and cried from the time he was stripped from his mother until he arrived on the steamboat. And even then he did not stop crying. The slave boy tried not to be affected by his whimpering and sullenness and tuned him out for much of their voyage.

On the two-day trip to New Orleans, Horatio found some fleeting comfort in a couple of hours of agitated sleep, jerking at any noise made by the chained coffle. The slave boy was relieved that Horatio had finally fallen off to sleep, giving him a few hours of peace, as much as could be found in the confined and cramped space that housed the multitude of heart-sick, bought-and-sold Negroes.

On their arrival in New Orleans, the slaves were carried to a slave pen at the back of the county courthouse. It was a small yard, containing several buildings, no more than twenty feet wide. The slaves were herded inside and finally allowed to eat. Horatio's new master fed his slaves well, better than most slaves generally were. Keeping them fed and healthy would ensure that he'd fetch a good price for his chattel. He provided them pork bacon, fish, cornmeal, and fresh water and milk. Horatio and the slave boy were seated in a corner of the building, still chained together, indulging on the meats and corn patties provided them. They were given enough to eat to satisfy their hunger until the auction began the following morning.

The slaves were kept in the buildings overnight where they slept chained to one another on damp and cold plank floors. The next day they were turned out into the yard to be inspected by would-be purchasers. They were kept there for one week, during which they were put up for sale, and many of the best stock sold at private auctions. Those not sold then were transported on to the next port and sold in a similar fashion.

It was not even daybreak when a Negro slave stood over Horatio and the slave boy as they slept. He nudged them and told them to wake up. Unchaining them, he motioned for them follow him to another room in the small building. Horatio was unsure if he should go with the strange man, looking questioningly at the slave boy, waiting for him to advise him of what to do.

"Move," he snapped, startling them both and shoving them into the room, causing Horatio to burst into tears.

The Negro slave shook Horatio to quiet him, causing him to whimper erratically, his small chest heaving uncontrollably from fear.

"You hush up, boy, or you goin' be whupped!" he yelled.

Horatio couldn't calm himself, his slim body shivering from fright. He wringed his hands and started crying even harder.

"Shut 'em up!" he ordered the slave boy. "Make 'em shut up or you goin' git whupped too."

The slave boy walked over to Horatio and leaned down, "All dat noise ya keepin' ain't goin' git me in no trouble. Ya bedder shut up. And stop dat cryin'."

Horatio noticed the evil glint in the boy's eye and stepped backward, blinking his widened eyes in disbelief. He felt the coldness of the slave boy's stare on his face, and the sting of his words gave him pause. Although the slave boy had made no attempt to befriend him, he had given Horatio some comfort on the trip. His presence and being chained to him for so long kept Horatio from feeling all alone in the world. But now he was alone.

"Git o'er dar and git washed up," the Negro slave ordered Horatio.

He moved hesitantly toward a waiting pot of water.

"Git his clothes off and wash 'em down," he ordered the slave boy who resented having to be bothered with a boy he did not know and did not want to assist.

He undressed Horatio and washed him down roughly with some greasy water as he had seen the slaveholders at the auction do the other slaves, including himself. Horatio winced in pain, his tender skin easily bruised by the coarseness of the oiled-soaked sackcloth, his moans and whimpers only exasperating the slave boy more.

"Quiet!" he shouted. "I don't wanna hear it no mo'."

Horatio heaved unsteadily, trying to bear the pain inflicted on him by the slave boy. He closed his eyes tightly and wished for his mother, hoping when he opened his eyes again, his wish would appear before him. He waited until the unwilling slave boy completed his task and then popped open his eyes, only to face disappointment. He forced back a tear and allowed the surge of anger welling up inside him to overpower him, pulling away from the slave boy and running toward the entrance of the building. The slave boy watched nervously, contemplating whether or not to warn the Negro slave whose back was to him. As Horatio reached the door, he slowed and looked back to see if anyone was following him, noticing the slave boy looking at him disapprovingly. He turned around and forced the door open, only to be stopped by another Negro standing guard outside the building's entrance.

"And were ya dink ya goin'?" he asked sharply, arresting Horatio's arm and tightening his grip on it.

"Lit me go!" Horatio screamed.

"I'll lit y'chu go alwight," the Negro guard snarled, pushing him back inside the building.

He was met by the Negro slave as he made his way to the entrance, "Git Mr. Thornwald. And take 'em to da block."

The Negro guard shoved Horatio into the Negro slave's hands and exited the building.

"Ya hankerin' for a whuppin', ain't cha? Well, dat's watcha goin' git," he growled, directing him back to the wash pot and pushing him to the floor.

"And you...ya gittin' five lashes fo' not watchin' 'em," the Negro slave pointed to the slave boy, who grew increasingly angry with having to be accountable for Horatio's actions. "Finish washin' 'em up."

The slave boy moved angrily toward Horatio who was huddled on the floor next to the wash pot, whimpering and trying to pacify himself. He refused to let the slave boy touch him again.

"If ya knows wat's good for ya, ya'll shut up all dat noise and do watcha told. I don't care if ya run 'way. Ya jus' ain't goin' git me lashed wit' cha," he warned, grabbing Horatio's arm and jerking him nearer to him.

He finished washing Horatio down more fiercely than before, Horatio wincing once again in pain.

Mr. Thornwald entered the building, followed by the Negro guard who pointed out Horatio.

"You's done done it now," the slave boy warned, watching cautiously as the man stood still, giving the Negro guard an order.

Horatio couldn't hear what Mr. Thornwald had said, but he sensed he should be afraid. He felt his body grow weak, and he wanted once again to run away. After Mr. Thornwald turned and left the building, the Negro guard rushed over to the Negro slave to tell him to get Horatio ready to go to the auction block.

"Put dis on 'em," the Negro slave ordered the slave boy, throwing a sackcloth shirt and a pair of pants on the floor next to them. "And grease his nappy head. Make 'em present'ble."

The slave boy dressed Horatio and did what he could to grease down Horatio's curly locks that had become disheveled and matted over the long voyage. He combed and pressed down with his hands the longest sections of his hair, not caring how rough he was on Horatio's tender head. After making Horatio look as presentable as he could, he hoped that would be the last he would have to see of him. Moments later the Negro slave took Horatio to the front of the building and lined him up in front of six other slaves, chaining them together, the sound of hard, cold metal clamping down around his ankles, startling him and sending him into another fit of tears.

"I ain't tellin' ya 'gin, boy. Shut dat damn fuss," the Negro slave ordered, Horatio trying to quiet himself, his body twitching in sporadic heaves.

An elderly Negro gentleman, chained to a young, thickly-built man, reached forward and patted Horatio on the shoulder to try to comfort him. He looked up hoping to see the face of his dear mother, but instead saw the aged countenance of a man that could have been his grandfather.

He leaned forward and whispered to Horatio, "Son, if ya shows dem buyers you's a strong li'l boy, dey won't harm ya. Stand up skraight, don't cry, and answer e'ry queshion dey ash ya like a big boy, and ya'll fare bedder. Ya dink ya can do dat?"

Horatio moaned, "I wanna go home ta muh mama," the sadness in his voice almost sending the elderly gentleman to tears.

"I knows ya do, son," he agreed. "We all want dat. Ta go home."

"D'ya know were she at?" Horatio asked, sensing some compassion from the stranger and hoping he could tell him something about his mother's whereabouts.

"No, son," he said forlornly. "Uhm 'fraid she prob'ly long gone fum y'ere."

He could hear the Negro guard outside calling for the first group of slaves to be sent out.

"It's time ta go out. Ya dink ya can do wat I told ya to?" he asked, gripping Horatio's slim shoulders and facing him forward.

Horatio nodded, the reassuring voice of a man he'd never seen before who felt compelled to show him a bit of compassion made him feel a little more resigned to his current situation.

The Negro slave walked to the front of the line of chained slaves and tapped on the door. The Negro guard opened the door and motioned for the chained coffle to head outside to the open yard about thirty feet to the right of the building in front of the county courthouse.

The line of slaves with washed faces and combed hair were ordered to form a line, standing side by side in front of spectators who had come to the yard to inspect them for purchase. Horatio stood next to the elderly gentlemen who whispered once again for him to do everything that was asked of him to ensure no ill treatment would befall him, and he agreed to do so. He stood as

20

straight as he could and looked as sprightly as his sad demeanor would allow.

Mr. Thornwald escorted several buyers out to the line of Negroes and issued them catalogues containing the identification number and descriptions of the slaves for purchase. Horatio was the first called.

"Step fo'ward," Mr. Thornwald ordered, his hellish voice startling him.

He looked up at the elderly Negro gentleman who nodded for him to obey. He took a couple of steps forward and stood upright as straight as he could.

Mr. Norris Brandenburg, a buyer from Texas, walked around him, looking him up and down. He pulled open his mouth to inspect his teeth to see how old he was.

"Still got his cuttin' teeth," Norris commented, gripping his slim arms and feeling for signs of fitness, Horatio stunned by the gentleness with which he handled him. "How old is ya?"

Horatio stood still afraid to answer. He wanted to look back at the elderly gentleman, but the man still had his arm in his grasp.

"I axed, how old is ya?" Norris inquired again.

Horatio refused to answer.

"Wat's wrong wit' 'em?" Cain't he talk?" Norris asked, knowing that slave traders normally teach their slaves to answer the questions asked of them, and he definitely wasn't in the market for a mute.

"He jus' be a li'l scared, why he won't speak," the elderly Negro gentleman interjected, and by the time he let the words roll off his tongue, he knew he had made one of the biggest mistakes of his life, a slave speaking when not spoken to.

"Who told *you* to speak?" Mr. Thornwald shouted, grabbing him by the arm and forcing him to the ground, his stiffened bones aching as he kneeled on one knee. He turned and motioned for the Negro guard to come forward, "Unchain 'em!"

The Negro guard unlocked his chains and quickly stepped backwards.

"Give me muh paddle," Mr. Thornwald ordered, the Negro guard removing a one-inch thick paddle, hung from his shoulder by a leather strap and made of hickory with eight penny-sized auger holes bored into it.

Mr. Thornwald ordered the elderly gentleman to strip his clothes. Then he ordered the Negro guard to tie his hands and to give him five lashes on his rear end, the corkscrew-shaped bits piercing his skin as the paddle made contact. The elderly man screamed in agony at each flogging, blood gushing from his rear end as the Negro guard made five swings against his flesh. When the Negro guard finished giving him the five lashes, he stepped backward, the image of the elderly man keeling over in pain having no effect on him.

"Git 'em cleaned up," Mr. Thornwald commanded and turned once again to Horatio who was visibly shaken by the violent display. "Da man ashed ya, how old you was."

The elderly Negro gentleman looked over at Horatio and nodded for him to comply, a pained smile befalling his face. He knew speaking when not spoken to would warrant a lashing, but he could not bear to watch a child that reminded him so much of his grandson who had been sold just months earlier be flogged right before him, which would have been Horatio's fate had he not spoken up. Horatio didn't understand why they beat the elderly man. He hadn't done anything wrong. He was simply nice to him.

Desperately trying to hold back tears, he eked out nervously, "Fo'."

The Negro guard dragged the elderly man back to the building and shoved him inside for the Negro slave to get him cleaned up and readied to be returned to the auction block.

Norris finished examining Horatio and asking of him what he desired to know and then bid two hundred and fifty dollars for him. Horatio was sold to him and was placed over to the side to wait for other slaves he would purchase. By the end of the auction, he had purchased eight slaves and had them bound together in chains to be taken to the docks to board the awaiting steamboat, this time heading to Galveston, in the Republic of Texas.

Almost immediately upon boarding the ship, Horatio, overcome by the gruesome scene he had witnessed at the auction, fell ill. By the time the steamboat made the two-day trip to Texas, he was near death and seemed to unlikely to recover. Fearing he may lose his investment, Norris directed his on-ship doctor to treat Horatio, but the doctor could not figure out what had caused him to fall ill.

When Horatio finally woke up after three days of being in a semi-conscious state, he was lying on a pallet on the floor of a slave cabin. He opened his eyes slowly, the brightness of the sunlight stinging the insides of his eyelids. His head was foggy, and he was feeling slightly disoriented. He didn't know where he was or how he had gotten there. He looked around the room, the stench of overcooked lard permeating the air of the small one-room cabin. The room reminded Horatio of his home at the Finnius plantation, a small room with two pallets laid on top of wooden planks to his left, a fireplace and the hand-hewn table with two benches to his left. Hearing voices, he turned to his right to see a Negro woman and man sitting at the hand-hewn table discussing his presence in their home. A few minutes later, the woman turned to him and noticed Horatio was awake.

"Well, hallo dar," the woman smiled. "Ya mus' be hungry."

She stood up and walked over to the fireplace in which a metal pot hung filled with rabbit stew. She filled a metal bowl full

24

of the mixture and broke off a piece of cornbread and walked over to his bed. The male Negro got up and walked over to him and stood over him, his massive size giving scare to Horatio, who cringed from the sight of him.

"It's okay, Horatio," the woman said. "Dis is yo' uncle."

Horatio paused, wondering how these people knew his name. Who were these people? Why was he here? Where was his mama? The questions raced through his mind, but he found it difficult to form the words to ask them the questions.

"And uhm ya aunt. Ya aunt Virginia. Aunt Virginny," the woman added.

"Hi son," the man said. "Uhm yo' Uncle Joe."

Horatio looked at the woman worriedly, wondering why he was with these people and not with his mother.

"Mama?" Horatio mumbled, looking around anxiously for her.

Aunt Virginny paused and looked up at her husband sadly, unsure of how to explain to him what had happened to his mother.

"Lit's git a li'l food in ya, boy," Aunt Virginny said quickly, trying to distract Horatio from his thoughts.

Horatio was hungry and did not want to turn down any food at this point. He sat up quickly as Aunt Virginny placed the bowl of rabbit stew on his lap. He clenched the spoon and dug into the stew with a passion, the warm, greasy broth warming his insides.

25

"He was hungry," Aunt Virginny said.

Horatio finished the bowl of stew and tore into the cornbread, biting off pieces too large to swallow without some effort to chew into small, digestible pieces. He washed down the sustenance with some warm milk that Uncle Joe had milked from one the cows on the plantation earlier in the day.

"Ya got ya fill, son?" Uncle Joe asked.

Horatio motioned for Aunt Virginny to give him some more stew, and she giggled lightly.

"Hum, he gotta appetite like yours, Joe," she laughed.

"I see dat," Uncle Joe replied, patting him lightly on the head.

Aunt Virginny filled the bowl with more stew and gave it to Horatio with another small piece of cornbread, Horatio gulping them down as quickly as he had the first.

"Alwighty den," Aunt Virginny said. "Ya dink we oughtta call fo' the massa since he 'wake?"

"Yeah, he wanted ta know as soon as he came to," Uncle Joe said. "I'll head to da Big House ta fetch 'em."

Uncle Joe hadn't been gone more than ten minutes before returning alone.

"Were he at?" Aunt Virginny asked curiously.

"He sent fo' da county doc ta come out. He should be here in da next couple hours," Joe replied. "He said ta keep 'em calm 'til den."

Horatio lay back on the pallet, staring at his Aunt Virginny and Uncle Joe, but he still didn't feel like they were family. He had never met them, and he didn't know why he was there. But for the moment he was feeling tired and drifted slowly off to sleep.

A couple of hours later, the county doctor who had come to inspect Horatio appeared at the door of the cabin with Norris. Uncle Joe opened the door and let them enter. Horatio was startled awake, and now was thoroughly unnerved, unsure of the treatment he would receive at the hands of this new master.

"I think this one'll survive," the doctor said after examining Horatio.

"What was wrong wit' 'em?" Norris asked.

"Nothin' physical that I can determine. I think it was a case of a broken heart," the doctor replied. "But keep an eye on 'em anyway. Just in case."

"We will," Aunt Virginny said.

Norris walked to the door with the doctor, asking, "Ya sure he'll be alright?"

"Looks like it. Sometimes young slaves taken from their mothers exhibit this kind of distress, and some don't overcome it. I think he'll fare just fine," he added.

"I just don't want my son to get too attached if the Negro boy won't survive," Norris said in a concerned tone.

"I understand," the doctor noted. "Keep me posted if anything changes."

"I will," Norris said, both he and the doctor walking outside of the slave cabin. "Thanks for comin' out and checkin' on him."

Uncle Joe waited for them to leave before closing the door behind them.

"Wat'd he mean by if he won't survive?" Aunt Virginny asked angrily.

"Ya know wat he meant," Uncle Joe replied sharply, contempt for Norris straddling his words as he recanted a previous incident. "Jus' like he did Henry's son wen he loss his arm in dat wagon acc'dent. He cuddn't pull his weight, so he sold 'em."

"We cain't lit dat happen to Horatio," Aunt Virginny said. "I will make sho my sister's son goin' survive."

Uncle Joe nodded, his expression showing he was not as sure of the boy's recovery as Aunt Virginny. The boy hadn't been awake but a couple of hours, and for the last two days ran a fever that was so high, they could have cooked bread on his forehead. Aunt Virginny spent day and night washing him down and wrapping potatoes on the bottom of his feet and under his armpits to draw out the fever, the potatoes turning black like tar. She even called the high conjure woman, Aunt Millie, to come see about him, and when she did appear, Aunt Millie called up spirits over him and told Aunt Virginny to sprinkle his head with some dust she had given her and to wait two days. Aunt Virginny, during that time, followed Aunt Millie's instructions, but she also tried every home-grown remedy she had remembered her mother and grandmother using to cure ailing patients.

Horatio fell asleep again and Aunt Virginny sat by his side, watching him, washing him down, and praying for his full recovery. Two days later, he was fully recovered. Aunt Virginny wasn't sure what did it, but she didn't discount Aunt Millie's role in the matter. Uncle Joe didn't know what cured Horatio either although he was skeptical of the conjure woman, believing she was bilking all of the slaves out of their hard-earned wages, what little they could scrounge up, and telling them a bunch of lies, keeping many of them so afraid of their own shadows that he could yell "Boo" to any of them and they would take off running through the woods like a spooked horse, only to be slowed down and stopped by sheer exhaustion.

Horatio was feeling much better than in the previous days, but still was not comfortable in his new surroundings. His Aunt Virginny fixed him a bowl of hominy and sweetened milk, which he gulped down. After eating, he sat on the pallet examining his new surroundings. Uncle Joe had gone out to the fields while Aunt Virginny stayed at the cabin to tend to him. It wouldn't be long before he would be taken up to the Big House to perform his duties for which he was bought. Aunt Virginny wanted to make sure he understood what was going to happen to him so that he would not feel afraid and be subject to the lash for disobedience.

"Horatio, ya know why ya was brought y'ere?" she asked.

He shook his head no, examining her thoughtful face, which seemed to mask years of pain and heartache, but her countenance seemed undisturbed by it.

"Well, I need ta tell ya wat ya goin' be 'spected ta do. Ya goin' be da servant to da massa son. Massa Victor," she began. "Ya know wat a servant do?"

Again he shook his head no.

"Well, ya goin' have ta do whatever da boy tell ya ta do," Aunt Virginny said. "He yo' massa. He own ya. Ya understand dat?"

Horatio once again shook his head no.

Aunt Virginny paused and then said, "Okay, ya 'parently don't understand. Lit me put it dis way. If ya don't do wat yo' massa tell ya to do, ya goin' git whupped. Do ya understand dat?"

Horatio quickly nodded his head yes and cringed before her.

"Oh no, baby. I ain't goin' whup ya. The massa goin' whup ya if ya don't do wat he say," she explained, leaning forward to calm him. "And dat's why uhm tellin' ya dis so dat ya know how ta ack 'round yo' massa. Do wat he say and ya goin' be alwight."

Horatio didn't like this arrangement. He didn't have to do what anybody said but his mother, and he wanted to know where she was.

30

"Mama?" Horatio asked pitifully.

"Yo' mama?" Aunt Virginny repeated. "Uh...yo' mama's gone, chile. Lawd knows were."

"I want muh mama," Horatio cried, tears filling his eyes.

"I know baby," Aunt Virginny said, hugging him. "I want ta see yo' mama too. I wish I could git her fo' ya. But I don't know were she at."

Her words gave little comfort to Horatio, but her warm embrace made him feel a little better. It wasn't his mother's warm bosom, but at least he didn't feel alone anymore.

"Look, dey'll be comin' fo' ya soon, so I need ta prepare ya ta render 'sistance to yo' massa. Ya'll need ta do wat dey tell ya so ya don't git whupped. Dat's da only way I know to protect ya, seein' dat I won't be wit' cha ta watch o'er ya. You's muh sister chile and I want ta make sho ya goin' be okay."

Horatio stopped crying and listened to her words. He wasn't sure what he was going to have to do, and he wasn't sure if he wanted to do it. He lay back on the pallet, wondering what he should do. The thought of escaping crossed his mind, but he had no idea of where he was or how to get back to his home, not even his home anymore since Mistress Finnius had sold off all the slaves on the plantation. Even if he wanted to go back there, he couldn't. In addition, he had no earthly idea of his mother's whereabouts. For now, he would have to resign himself to his current fate, whatever that may be.

The next day, Norris sent for Horatio, and Aunt Virginny escorted him to the Big House. They entered the foyer and Rubeline, the head cook, showed them to the parlor where Norris was seated.

"Massa Brand'nburg," Aunt Virginny said, "y'ere Horatio as ya r'quested."

"Oh, fine, Virginny," Norris said. "Rubeline, git my boy in y'ere."

Rubeline nodded and disappeared, returning a few minutes later with a pale faced, red-headed boy only a year Horatio's junior.

"Come hither, Victor," Norris said. "I have somethin' fo' ya."

"Yes, Papa?" Victor said walking eagerly toward his father.

"This is yo' man servant," Norris said.

"But Papa, I'm not a man," Victor said.

"Not yet," Norris chuckled. "But yo' man servant's gonna ensure ya turn into a right fine one."

Norris motioned for Horatio to step forward. Aunt Virginny nudged him, but he hesitated to move. Then she leaned down and whispered in his ear, "'Member wat I told ya would happen if ya didn't obey?"

With those words, Horatio immediately stepped forward and stood before Norris who sized him up for his son.

"He'll make a fine servant," Norris said. "Don't ya think so, son?"

"Can I play wit' 'em?" Victor asked, paying little attention to the reasoning his father had purchased Horatio.

"Yes. He's yours to do wit' as ya please," Norris replied.

Aunt Virginny wasn't too comfortable with that last statement. She knew how the boy had been allowed to run wild around Hollow Creek. No older than he was, he was already a little terror to the other slave children on the plantation, and with a father who was going to allow the boy to have absolute authority over Horatio, it gave her great concern. She watched as the two boys started to run past her to go outside to play.

"Hold up son," Norris said, halting them. "Lit's git 'em settled in his room first."

"Okay, Papa," Victor said.

"Rubeline has yo' room prepared. She's in the kitchen," he said, sending Victor and Horatio in there.

Aunt Virginny watched as the boys exited the room, and then she started to head back to her cabin but was stopped by Norris.

"Virginny," he said, standing up and walking toward her. "My wife's goin' need some more help 'round y'ere."

"Yessur?" Aunt Virginny said.

"I wantcha ta help Rubeline 'round the house. Ya can also make sure the boy learns his role," he said.

"Oh, sur. Yes. I be glad ta take on dose duties," she answered, knowing this would allow her to keep an eye on Horatio and ensure he fared well.

"I've already talked with Rubeline, and she'll fill ya in on whatcha are to do 'round here," he added.

"I will, sur," she said and turned to head to the kitchen. She got to the door of the parlor and paused, "Sur, may I axe a queshion of dee?"

"Yes, Virginny?" he said.

"Do ya have any word of muh sister Clareene?" she asked, knowing that he and her sister had liaisons, which produced their son, Horatio.

Stunned, Norris paused. He had not seen Clareene since the auction but often wondered how she was faring. He wanted to bid on her, but did not because his aunt had promised Clareene to her cousin in Georgia. His aunt did allow him to purchase Horatio as a gift for his son.

"No. All I know is she was sold to a buyer from Georgia," Norris replied, lowering his head and shaking it.

"So she alwight den?" she asked.

"As far as I know," he answered.

"Dank ya, sur," Aunt Virginny said and exited the room.

Aunt Virginny met with Rubeline who filled her in on what she would be doing, and she began working that same day and didn't get back to her cabin until well after dark. When she did arrive home, Uncle Joe was waiting for her, irritated with the unexpected change.

"Were ya been all day?" he asked, seated in front of the fireplace smoking a pipe.

"Massa decided ta have me work in the kitchen wit' Rubeline," she answered, her body tired and aching.

"Dat's jus' da beginnin'," he said angrily.

"Watcha mean by dat?" she retorted, offended by the insinuation.

"Ya know how he is," he replied sharply. "Wen he git da notion…."

"Well, he ain't gettin' no notion wit' me," Aunt Virginny returned, sensing Uncle Joe's uneasiness with the arrangement, knowing that was how Norris and her sister began their liaisons. She also was in no mood for an argument that was obviously going to happen if she didn't squash the subject because she knew Uncle Joe was frustrated that Norris wielded so much control over their lives. Over all the slaves' lives at his plantation, Hollow Creek.

"Ya know dis mean we ain't goin' see mucha each other," Uncle Joe moaned. "Rubeline and her hubband ain't seen each other in months."

"But he live on da Horton plantation. His massa won't lit nunna his slaves see dar wives but two or twee times a year," she said. "At least we y'ere. Together."

"For now," Uncle Joe noted irritably, turning back toward the fireplace and puffing hard on his pipe, feeling that every change

35

Norris made with his slaves, even the decision to sell a slave, meant they were less empowered to do anything about it. There were several slave families at Hollow Creek that had been devastated by the decision of their master to sell off one of the slaves for profit or for paying off some indebtedness.

"I know honey," she said, walking over to him and kissing him softly on the cheek.

BASTARD SLAVE

Early that morning Evan rode into town on horse-drawn wagon, passing three men sitting on benches outside Putnam's General Store. They eyed Evan intensely, and Evan returned the same.

He pulled up to the front of the Post Office. The men talked among themselves, but their demeanor concerned Evan. Something about the men didn't set well with him. And one of the men he thought he knew. Still watching the men, he got down and tied the horses to the fence post and went inside. He returned shortly and walked to the General Store to buy some supplies. He passed the men as he entered the store. While talking with the owner, he watched the men through the dusty pane glass window. Then he exited the store and headed toward his wagon.

"Don't we know you?" one man asked.

Carrying two sacks, Evan stopped and responded, "I don't think so," and continued walking toward his wagon.

"Ain't you that fella that inherited all that land out past Hollow Creek?" the second man retorted.

"Naw...ain't you the slave that stole that land?" a third man corrected, his face hidden behind his low-hanging, shapeless, rawhide hat.

Evan hesitated, knowing the line of questioning these men were leveling at him would lead to nothing but trouble. They were the type of men that hankered for a fight. All they needed was a reason to start trouble, and they usually found it.

"I don't know what y'all talkin' 'bout. I got business to tend to," Evan said, ignoring the man's last comment and heading to his wagon to unload the sacks.

"You hear that fellas? He got business to tend to," the third man said. "I guess he too important to talk with us po' white folk."

Evan recognized the voice of the third man. He didn't want any trouble, so he hurried to untie the horses and got on the wagon. Then he headed down the road in the direction he had come.

Later that afternoon, Evan was working in his corn field in the midday heat. He stood up to wipe his forehead drenched in sweat with the sleeve of his denim shirt. He saw a figure on horseback, distorted by the scorching sun, riding up the path to his house. As the figure got closer, Evan recognized the man, the same man at the General Store. It was the wiry, bitter Henry. He hadn't seen him in a couple of years. Henry stopped short of the path leading to Evan's house, just as Evan met him.

"What'd'ya want?" Evan asked sharply.

"Is that any way to greet an ole friend?" Henry asked slyly, the familiarity of his voice grating on Evan's skin.

"You ain't never been no friend of mine. What'd'ya want?" Evan repeated.

"I came to claim what's rightfully mine," Henry answered boldly.

"What's rightfully yours?" Evan asked piercingly.

"Hell yeah. All this should be mine," Henry said, extending his arm as if painting a picture of Evan's property.

"Not by the law, it ain't," Evan said coldly.

"We'll see about that," Henry answered defiantly.

"I got this property legally," Evan said confidently, now noticing Henry's attention had been diverted elsewhere.

"I see you got a nice little family here. Right fine woman there," Henry said, noticing Evan's wife Emile and the children watching from the kitchen window. "I bet she's a good roll in the hay, ain't she?"

Henry looked back at the house to see Emile watching them. His body ran hot with anger.

"Say another word 'bout my wife and you'll regret it," Evan snarled.

"Tain't no use in getting' yo' britches in a bunch. I was just commentin'...," Henry said, before being cut off by Evan.

"You can keep yo' comments to yo'self," Evan snapped, stepping toward him.

Unaffected, Henry shouted, "I'll say what I damn well please. And I'll do what I damn well please. And if I wanted to, I could take that wife of yours and make her kiss my ass with you watchin' ...."

Before Henry could finish the statement, Evan had lunged at him and pulled him from the horse. He started wailing on Henry, beating him with a fierceness and intensity, partly because of the disrespect Henry had shown him over the years, but mainly because Evan didn't like him.

Emile saw the commotion and ran out of the house. Evan had beaten Henry severely, and to Emile it looked like he would kill him.

She stopped at the porch and yelled out, "Evan! Stop!"

Evan heard her cry and paused momentarily. Henry used the moment to wince himself away from Evan's grip. He backed up, his legs pushing up a cloud of dust as his body propelled backwards.

"You crazy bastard!" Henry shouted. "You gonna regret this, slave!"

"I ain't no slave no mo'. Now get the hell off my property," Evan growled, inching towards Henry, his fists still clinched.

Henry, giving Evan a contemptuous stare, grabbed his dusty rawhide hat and stood up, brushing dirt and debris from his shirt and trousers. He mounted his horse and headed down the path the way he had come.

Emile rushed to Evan, "You alright?"

"I'm fine," he said angrily, watching in disgust as Henry rode out of sight.

"What did he want?" she asked worriedly, examining his hand, which was bleeding.

"He claim this property's his," Evan replied coldly.

"But yo' papa willed it to you," she said. "And the judge ruled it legally bindin'."

"I know, but that damn fool Henry ain't gettin' that through his thick skull," Evan replied angrily.

Henry never liked Evan because his papa, Everette, who was married to Henry's aunt, had had an affair with one of his slaves, which produced his only son, Evan. When his wife discovered his infidelity, she was livid. Over time, they managed to work through their problems, but when Evan was a young teen, he came to work on his papa's plantation. To make matters worse, his papa showed more partiality toward his slave son than toward his own daughters.

Henry had overheard stories from his papa, Francois, about Everette's adoration of Evan. It agitated his wife, but Everette didn't seem to care. Francois would call Everette a fool for putting too much stock in that boy, whether or not he was his son. He was still a bastard and a slave. And Henry felt the same way.

Shortly after Evan arrived at Everette's plantation, he had had several run-ins with the teenaged Henry who also worked for Everette. Henry would test Evan just to see if he could get him riled up. He would taunt him out of earshot of Everette, but Evan always held his cool. After several weeks of taunting, Henry initiated a fight with Evan in the fields one day. Henry waited until Everette got down the corn row far enough not to notice his antics, and then he threw a clod of dirt at the back of Evan's head. The first time it hit him, Evan turned and stared heatedly at Henry, watching as Henry bawled over with laughter. Then Henry waited for Evan to turn back and threw another clod of dirt at his back. This time Evan, pushed to his limit, turned and ran toward Henry, knocking him to the ground and threatening him.

"Boy, I'll slit yo' throat from sun up to sun down if you touch me again," Evan growled, pinning Henry down on the ground, his forearm pressed against his throat.

"Get off me!" Henry shouted in a strangled voice, trying to pry Evan's arm from his throat.

"You touch me again, and you'll regret it," Evan reiterated, releasing the pressure from Henry's throat.

"You bastard," Henry growled as he managed to break away from him.

"I might be a bastard, but mess with me again, and this bastard'll slit yo' throat in yo' sleep," he added.

Fearful of Evan, Henry told his papa about the incident, causing Evan to get five lashes with the whip for attacking him. Evan took the punishment like a man—Evan still bared the scars from that lashing. From that point on Henry left Evan alone. He still never liked Evan. In fact, he despised him mainly because when Everette died years later, he willed the plantation and the land surrounding it to Evan. Henry was bitter about that and felt the plantation should have gone to his aunt's side of the family before going to Everette's "bastard slave" son.

Although Henry had left, he wasn't the type to let an issue go. Evan knew that Henry was a prideful man, and he would most likely return, and not necessarily alone, so Evan prepared himself for possible retaliation. That afternoon he sent Emile and the children to Josiah Milner's farm to spend the night. He didn't want them there if Henry decided to seek revenge. Emile left hesitantly, telling Evan to be careful.

Evan waited for him with a pistol and a shotgun readied at his side, prepared for a second round with him. But Henry did not return that night. The following day Emile and the children returned home. Evan still wasn't comfortable with her home because he knew men like Henry. They were like rabid dogs. Once they set their sights on something, they would not let go until they were shot dead where they stood.

Three nights later, Evan awoke to the smell of smoke.

"Get up, Emile," Evan said firmly, nudging her awake.

Disoriented, she asked, "What?"

"I smell smoke. Get up and I'll get the girls," he said, pulling on his overalls and heading out of the bedroom to find out where the smoke was coming from.

Emile pulled on a dress and followed behind him. Evan went to Marie Claire's room and woke her up. He looked around for Mariah, their youngest daughter, but didn't see her.

"Where Mariah?" he asked Marie Claire who was barely awake.

She shrugged her shoulders and rubbed her eyes, unsure of what was going on. Evan picked her up and rushed downstairs with her and decided to take her outside to Emile instead of looking for Mariah. He would come back inside to find her.

Emile screamed when she realized he had not gotten Mariah out of the house.

"Where Mariah?" she asked, running toward them and taking Marie Claire from his arms.

"I don't know," he said anxiously.

44

Emile started to run back inside to get her daughter, but Evan stopped her.

"No. Stay with Marie Claire. I'll get her."

He turned back and ran toward the house, which was now engulfed in flames. He paused, wondering where Mariah could have gone. Lately, she had been waking up in the middle of the night and going to her favorite place to sleep, on the floor in front of the fireplace in the downstairs parlor. When he realized where she might be, he rushed back inside. At first he could not get to the parlor. Then he managed to crawl under some fallen debris and saw her. She was still asleep. He lifted her small body and headed outside.

Emile screamed in agony when she saw Evan carrying her limp baby girl, their faces mottled with soot and ash.

"Is she dead?" Emile cried, running to him and wrapping her arms around the child.

"No, she alive," he said softly, giving her the child and hugging her.

Emile fell into his arms and sobbed horribly. Evan stood there, trying to console his wife and children, his house consumed by billows of grey smoke and roaring yellow flames.

Then he noticed something in the dirt path leading up to the house. He walked over to it and paused. It was a dusty rawhide hat, the same hat Henry wore when he came to his house the other day. He leaned down and picked it up, vowing under his breath, "I'm gonna kill that sumbabitch if it's the last thing I do."

That night Evan, filled with anger and revenge, took his family back to the Milner's farm. The next evening he set out to find Henry with the purpose of slitting his throat, to finish a job he should have done a long time ago. He rode into town to the local saloon, Ragin' Pete's, Henry's regular stomping ground, and waited outside for Henry to come out. Leaning against a post outside the Putnam's General Store, Evan had planned to attack him when he was alone, away from a crowd. However, while waiting for him, a brawl broke out inside the saloon, instigated by the loud-mouth, trash-talking Henry, who had accused a renowned gunslinger of cheating at poker.

"This ain't right," Henry yelled, his breath reeking of numerous shots of rotgut whiskey. "He cheated!"

"You callin' me a cheat?" the man growled, eyeing Henry coldly.

"Them cards ain't lyin'," Henry retorted cockily.

"You sayin' I cheated?" the man repeated, placing his hand on his gun.

"Alright fellas," a third man at the table interjected, trying to keep the peace.

"Naw, he called me a cheat," the man said. "I ain't lettin' nobody get away with callin' me a cheat."

46

Evan heard the commotion from outside and stood at full attention to listen out for what was going on. Then he heard one-sentence shouts, angry utterances, and several pleas from other patrons, trying to calm the man down.

A gunshot rang out.

Evan moved closer to the saloon with his gun ready in case Henry tried to make a getaway. Shortly after, Evan saw the man Henry had called a cheat exiting the saloon through the swinging saloon doors. Then two men dragged an innocent bystander's lifeless body outside and waited for the sheriff. The saloon crowd was stunned momentarily, but this not-uncommon act only brought pause to the lively vibrancy of the saloon crowd. They resumed their revelry to the level they had before the shooting.

Henry remained inside, talking trash and bragging about running off the man who cheated. It would be another hour before Henry would exit the saloon. When he did, it was dark, and Evan was prepared to exact his revenge. Henry, full of rotgut whiskey, stumbled off alone to his awaiting room at Madame Gypsy's boarding house.

Evan followed behind Henry. Slowly. Silently. Unnoticed.

When Henry arrived at the boarding house, he made his way up the stairs and stood at the door fumbling with the lock. Evan eased up the stairs behind him, the stairway lit dimly by the lamppost at the front of the boarding house. Henry finally got the lock opened and entered the room. He pulled off his shirt and kicked off his boots. Before he could take a second step, Evan grabbed him by his neck from behind, pulling Henry's body backwards and then wrapping his arm around Henry's neck and squeezing tightly, Henry struggling to grasp Evan's arms but unable to sustain a grip, Evan's arms tightening even more and lifting Henry's drunken body off the floor, his breath escaping from him, his eyes bulging from the pressure and forcing tears from them, his face reddening and then growing pale, then blue, his hands falling limp, his body giving way to death.

Evan continued to squeeze tightly until he was sure he had expunged all life from Henry's body, allowing his corpse fall to the floor. Evan stood over Henry's body, examining it for any signs of life. When he was sure of his demise, Evan walked toward the door.

Taking one last look back, he said, under his breath, "Bastard," and exited the room, closing the door behind him.

GRANDPA'S COURTSHIP

It was early on a Saturday morning, and Horace, Jason, and Buddy were working in the corn fields. It was late spring, and they were planting the season's corn crop. A mule led the plow, which Horace navigated, making furrows. His grandson Buddy came behind him, dropping corn in the furrows, and Horace's hired farmhand Jason would follow, covering the corn, all of them continuing this process for the next row and the next and the next until a huge field of corn was laid, time-consuming work that would make Horace consider giving up the trade every season when he'd think about how much work it would take to plant a field of corn.

They had just finished setting a row of corn, trying to finish by mid-morning, and were heading toward the other end of the row near the road that led to the local colored Baptist church when they saw a stout figure, distorted by jagged rays of sunlight, heading toward them. They stopped abruptly, wondering who it was, a hand waving in the air, the figure talking to the wind as it barreled down the corn row, a fireball of dust trailing behind it. As the figure got closer, Horace recognized it. It was Miss Margaret, and she was fired up mad.

"Horace Johnson!" she yelled. "If I ain't never seen a man so hard-nosed set in his stubborn-as-a-mule and mean-as-an-ass ways, I would never in my lifetime see it!"

Jason and Buddy were stunned at first, but they knew why Miss Margaret laid into Horace. Horace had no warning, so he couldn't get away before he was barraged by verbal assaults from the irritated colored woman.

"You are the stubbornest, orneriest, crankiest, belligerent, ill-tempered, crabbiest, cantankerousest, grouchiest, old negro...," Miss Margaret added before being cut off.

"Miss Margaret...now... Miss Margaret, I ain't gone be no more of your negroes," Horace interjected.

"Loud-mouthed, quarrelsome, grumpy, tetchy, surly...," she continued.

"Now, Miss Margaret, you better tell me what's got your panties in a pinch," Horace said sternly.

Jason and Buddy burst out laughing, which only angered the irate woman.

50

"You dirty, old letch!" Miss Margaret yelled. "How dare you use such devilish, sinful, vile, despicable, wicked language with me?"

And as quickly as Miss Margaret came down the corn row, she turned on her heels and left in a blur, leaving Horace speechless. Jason and Buddy bawled over in laughter.

"What y'all laughing at?" Horace said irritably, watching as Miss Margaret made her way angrily down the corn row, her floral print dress swaying from side to side in unison with the determined stride of her hefty hips.

"You!" Jason retorted, letting out a deep guffaw.

"Hush up, you fools!" Horace yelled. "Get back to work!"

Jason nudged Buddy in the side, both of them still overcome with laughter.

"I said, get back to work!" Horace repeated angrily, slapping the mule on the hind parts and shouting, "Gitty up! You stubborn ass!"

Jason and Buddy burst into another fit of laughter, annoying Horace even more.

"I don't know what the hell you two find so damn hilarious," Horace snapped.

"Now, Horace," Jason said, trying to hold back a snicker. "You know good and well what that was all about."

"I don't know what you talking 'bout," Horace said, turning his back to Jason.

"Oh, you don't, huh?" Jason mocked. "You know Miss Margaret been waiting for you to ask her to that church picnic all month long. And you stood around and acted like you didn't have no idea. The picnic is this afternoon, and I think she's trying to give you a hint. A big hint."

Horace paused, blinking his eyes and frowning, turning to Jason and asking, "You serious?"

"You mean you didn't know?" Jason asked, surprised by Horace's reaction.

"No," Horace replied.

"She been telling my wife about it all month. I guess that was my cue to tell you about it," Jason said, now realizing how angry Miss Margaret must have been.

Buddy said softly, "She mentioned it to me, but she never said to tell you anything, Grandpa."

Horace, irritated and needing someone to blame, snapped at Buddy, "Boy, why didn't you tell me?"

"Don't blame the boy," Jason said, defending Buddy. "You know she been sweet on you, and you been acting like you can't see it. Everybody in the whole county could see how she feel about you. But you. And this picnic was your chance to make your move."

Trying to regain his composure, Horace paused and then said, "How the hell that woman think I can read minds? She act like I'm supposed to know that's what she wanted. A woman gotta tell a man something. Women can't expect us to know what they want, when they want it, and how they want it."

Jason and Buddy stood quietly as Horace went on his own tirade, slapping the mule again on the hind parts.

"And another thing," Horace added. "She can't just come up to a man and fuss him out like he ain't nothing…."

Jason and Buddy followed behind Horace, snickering under their breaths.

Horace continued, "…talking to him any kind of way and expecting him to know what she all up in a tether about. Womenfolk. They so confused. And they trying to confuse everybody else."

"Horace, you know what you gotta do," Jason said, still smirking.

"Humph," Horace grunted and continued down the corn row, slapping the mule again on the hind parts to make it move.

Later that afternoon, a few hours before the church picnic was to take place, Horace hurried to get dressed in his best Sunday clothes, a dark grey suit, a round hat, and black shoes. He walked down the stairs and stopped in front of the mirror to inspect himself. He felt reasonably comfortable with how he looked although he hated wearing suits. But for this occasion, he felt he needed a little extra ammunition to combat his angry adversary, Miss Margaret.

He got into his horse-drawn wagon and headed to Miss Margaret's home. When he arrived, he paused, sitting on the wagon, trying to muster up the courage to face her. Then he got down and walked to her front door. Knocking firmly, he stepped back and adjusted his collar, preparing for another barrage of verbal attacks. Miss Margaret came to the front door and stood with her arms crossed, in irritation.

"Miss...Miss Margaret?" Horace stammered, taking off his hat and holding it nervously in his hands.

"Yes, Mr. Johnson," she replied tersely.

"Uh...I...Uh," Horace stuttered.

"What do you want, Mr. Johnson?" Miss Margaret snapped. "I ain't got all day."

Before Horace could stop himself, he let out how he truly felt in one breath, stating emphatically, "Well, if you'd shut your mouth for a dang minute, woman, you'd know I was here to apologize for not asking you to the church picnic and to say how beautiful you look right now and how beautiful I think you always look and how wonderful you can sing and how you drive me nuts with your crazy, foolish, feisty, moody, hollering ways!"

Miss Margaret was stunned at the revelation she had been praying for, for many months.

"Thank you, Lord," she whispered under her breath.

"What you say, woman?" Horace asked irritably, thinking she had again bad-mouthed him. "I just spilled my guts to you, and this is how you...."

"Oh, shut up, you ole fool, and come on inside," Miss Margaret said, tearing up and pushing open the screened door.

Taken aback, Horace stepped inside and was greeted with a soft peck on the cheek.

"What's that for?" Horace asked.

"For you being you," Miss Margaret said sweetly and escorted him to the parlor.

Horace stopped at the door, nervously examining the lavishly decorated room, plush furniture covered in washable covers for protection, a large rug covering hard wood floors, intricately designed, lace curtains at the window, a fireplace mantel dressed with flowers and greenery, a black lacquer piano with a tall, silver candelabra at its center, and a dark, mahogany wood chest that converted into a folding bed for guests. He especially admired the ornate rocking chair to the right, similar to the one his dead wife Emile had loved to sit in and rock her babies to sleep.

Miss Margaret was a widow, her husband having died of typhoid fever six years earlier. It took a long time for Miss Margaret to even think of finding another suitable husband. When she met Horace, something about him intrigued her. Even though he didn't attend church, she still considered him a good prospect for a companion because she believed the Lord had sent him her way and He would "convert" Horace in due time. In the meantime, she believed the Lord meant for her to follow this path, for if she did not follow God's Divine Plan, she would not be a good Christian woman.

"Would you like something to drink?" Miss Margaret asked.

"Yes, ma'am," Horace replied.

Miss Margaret left and returned with a serving tray, carrying a teapot, two cups, and a large slice of her homemade boysenberry pie. She set the tray down on the coffee table and sat on the sofa.

"Sit, Mr. Johnson," she said, motioning for him to be seated, Horace sitting down across from her.

She poured a cup of tea and passed it to him and then handed him a plate of boysenberry pie.

"Oh, Miss Margaret, you didn't need to go through all that trouble," Horace said politely.

"It was no trouble. Please, help yourself," she replied, giving him a fork.

He set his tea down and took a huge bite of the pie.

"Miss Margaret," he said, a burst for fruit flavor exciting his palate. "This is wonderful."

"Oh, thank you," she said pleasingly. "There's more where that came from."

"This is quite a plenty," he answered, finishing the slice of pie and enjoying it thoroughly.

Miss Margaret smiled.

"Thank you, again," he said, sipping on the hot tea to cleanse his palate.

"When was the last time you had a home-cooked meal?" she asked.

"Well," Horace began, thinking back. "Actually, it's been some years."

"How 'bout you come by next week and I cook a good, filling meal for you?" she said. "You need some sustenance working in those fields all day long."

"Well, how can I say no to such a nice proposition?" Horace replied, finishing the last of his tea. "Yes, I will be much obliged."

"Well, Mr. Johnson, I will need to get myself fixed up if I am going to make that picnic," she said, standing up.

Horace stood and said, "I'll be back at four to escort you."

"I will be waiting," she replied, walking him to the door.

Horace left and headed back to his home. He went into the house to see Buddy sitting at the kitchen table, eating some country ham and biscuits Horace had made for lunch.

"Where have you been?" Buddy asked, wondering why he was dressed up.

"If you must know, I'm escorting Miss Margaret to the church picnic today," Horace replied.

"That's three hours from now. Why you dressed so early?" Buddy asked with a smirk on his face.

"I didn't want to be late," Horace said irritably, seeing Buddy snickering. "That answer your question?"

Buddy laughed and threw up his hands in surrender, watching Horace storm upstairs like an ill-tempered child.

FACES IN THE WALL

The year 1914 brought with it many changes. World War I had begun in Europe, halting all commerce overseas. The European forces needed war supplies that they couldn't produce all on their own and sought the support of the United States to manufacture goods and supplies for the war effort.

Northern industries provided the war goods to Europe, but as demand grew, factories, mills, and mines required a new supply of labor. When labor agents from the northern cities paraded into Mississippi, promising employment with better wages than could be found in the South and free railroad fare provided for colored men and women alike, many uprooted their families and headed north.

White planters, who resented the massive exodus, a loss for them of cheap labor, rallied together to stop the mass departure.

One tactic used was barring coloreds from buying railroad tickets. Another tactic was enforcing the Pig Laws, many colored men being trotted off to jail for the most menial of offenses, leaving behind their wives and children to carry on the farm work in their absence. Those who couldn't flee to the North were forced to work for white wealthy farmers for meager wages or face jail and be forced to work for free.

Ton Stone was one of many fortunate ones who decided to leave Mississippi for a chance at a better life in Detroit. Ton Stone's parents had been forced into foreclosure and lost their farm and were struggling to make ends meet. When the labor agents came to town, his papa went to one of their rallies and was promised a job. He told Ton Stone about signing on, and he did. It was hard for them to leave their homes and friends, but with the growing racial tension and backward laws that subjugated coloreds even more than in the past, they saw no other option but to get out of the South and hope for new, less oppressive, living conditions.

Ton Stone stopped by Buford Tee's house to tell him that he and his family were planning to leave in a day after they finished clearing up some financial issues. Buford Tee was saddened to see Ton Stone leave, but he understood why.

"Man, I hate you going," Buford Tee said, sitting down on the porch steps and Ton Stone following suit.

"I wish it won't the way it is. But you know, man, my family can't make it down here," Ton Stone said. "Look at how many colored families done had to give up everything they ever worked for in this county alone. It don't make no sense, a colored man can't never catch a break."

"That's why I'm gone fight this damn system," Buford Tee snarled. "I'm gone make this damn system work for me."

"Well, you got a chance. August set you up right," Ton Stone said, an envious tone straddling on his words.

"It ain't about my grandpa," Buford Tee said angrily, irritated that Ton Stone did not have the same breaks he had had in life. "It's about playing the white man's game and beating him at his own fucked up rules."

"Well, you have fun playing the game. And I hope you win, but for me and my family, the game's over," Ton Stone said somberly.

They sat on the front steps of the porch talking more about their plans for the future, Buford Tee promising to visit as soon as Ton Stone was settled, and Ton Stone promising to return home and buy up his papa's property as soon as he made it big time.

"My papa ain't trying to come back here. He's seen so much, and he's tired of it," Ton Stone said.

"It get like that sometimes, Bro'," Buford Tee said.

"I'm coming back," Ton Stone said firmly. "I'm coming back and buying up my papa's property. It's been in the family for years, and I ain't letting it go that easy."

"I'm gone sell more whiskey than any colored man ever sold in this county. In this state. Hell, in this country. Watch me," Buford Tee boasted.

Ton Stone looked at Buford Tee pensively, knowing when they set their minds to doing something, they always made it happen. And they were going to make this happen.

"We gone do this, ain't we?" Ton Stone said excitedly.

"Hell yell, we gone do this," Buford Tee said. "In five years, we gone do this. Agreed?"

"Agreed," Ton Stone said, accepting his challenge.

Later that evening Buford Tee and Ton Stone headed to the barrelhouse to celebrate Ton Stone's last night in Mississippi. The barrelhouse, called the Hankering by the local colored patrons, was a long dwelling, constructed much like the shotgun housing seen on the plantations of many wealthy farmers who profited from prison labor in Mississippi.

The Hankering was located down by the railroad in Wayne County, open only on weekends, the only time most coloreds had off work. It was a place for them to get away from weightiness of the workweek, and particularly, from their white employers, to enjoy a night or two of drinking, of course, but gambling, a little sex, or rather a lot of sex, and dancing also satisfying the desires of the patrons.

Locals made their way to the Hankering in a variety of ways, on horseback, by horse-drawn wagon loaded down with patrons, and even on tractors, on loan for the evening from their employers, pulling flatbed trailers filled with men and women desiring an evening of unbridled pleasure and unadulterated entertainment.

The deputy of Wayne County and some of his officers would sit in their Model T Ford squad cars, watching as the colored folk made their way to the barrelhouse. They'd wait until an hour before midnight to raid the place, when most folks were torn down from drunkenness, and as they put it, involving themselves in all manner of sin and debauchery.

A piano player beat out tunes on the old Steinway piano as colored men and women in their best going out clothes, women in fitted dresses designed to attract the attention of their male suitors and the men in clean shirts and dungarees, worn only for a night out on the town, strutted their stuff on the wooden plank dance floor, jiggling and twisting, bopping and dipping, their unrestrained dance movements ignited by the lightning bolt effects of the bootleg liquors and beers they consumed.

The owner would set out a barrel of bootleg whiskey and a chock barrel of the homemade beer, and men and women with tin cups would dip them in the barrel and partake of the mind-numbing, sense-altering brews. One or two cups would set them up right, but more than that would knock them out. Most folks could handle one or two cups, but not too many could handle much more than that, although many had tried. Those crazy enough to test their mettle would fall prey and be sidelined against the wall of the barrelhouse until the effects wore off; oftentimes, it'd be late the next day before they would make their way back home.

Some patrons made use of their time at the barrelhouse by gambling in the back of the joint, shooting craps, playing Head and Tail and Two Up, and Three Card Monte, and some betting a gig at one hundred to one odds, bets as low as a penny being placed, hopeful gamblers wishing for the big pay out, their hopes often dashed as the odds often favored the barrelhouse owners.

Buford Tee had never been to the Hankering before, but Ton Stone had. They entered the smoked-filled sweatbox already alive with bumping piano playing, energetic and uninhibited dancing, and more liquor than the law allowed, the floors covered with the intense, fiery potion.

The minute Buford Tee sat down, he spotted a young, strikingly beautiful, Creole woman, her face the color of the sun and her hair, the texture of finely weaved silk.

Buford Tee nudged Ton Stone, "Hey, man, check her out."

Ton Stone knew the woman. And he knew her husband. Her ex-husband, but still her man in every sense of the word.

"You don't want to mess with that," Ton Stone warned.

"Why, what's up with her?" Buford Tee asked. "You and her got…."

"Naw, man. I just know she come with a lot of baggage. Baggage no man want to carry," Ton Stone replied.

"What you mean?" Buford Tee asked, still mesmerized by her beauty.

"She taken," Ton Stone said. "And any man that look at her…."

Buford Tee had temporarily tuned out Ton Stone who realized he was looking at trouble.

"The way you looking at her now. Something that fine, ain't nothing but trouble," Ton Stone added.

"Man, you make too much out of rumors. I don't see no man 'round her," Buford Tee said, preparing to make his move her way.

"Look, you crazy if you step to her. Her man crazy. The kind of crazy that'll kill you and think nothing of it," Ton Stone cautioned.

"Where he at?" Buford Tee asked.

Ton Stone looked around but didn't see him anywhere.

"I don't see him, but you can best believe he got his eyes watching her," Ton Stone said, pointing toward the bouncer standing at the front of the joint.

"Well, ain't no harm in saying hello," Buford Tee said, standing up and heading her way.

He walked over to Miss Carmelia, who was working behind the counter serving whiskey and beer to the patrons.

"How do?" Buford Tee said, smiling.

Miss Carmelia looked up at him and nodded and resumed her duties, washing shot glasses and cleaning off the bar countertop, a pine wood structure that seated four people. Buford Tee sat on the bar stool and watched her work.

"Can I get a shot of whiskey?" Buford Tee asked.

Miss Carmelia poured a shot and slid it over to him, all without giving him a glance.

"Fifty cents," she said, continuing to clean the shot glasses.

Buford Tee gulped it down and shook his head. The brew was more potent than what his grandfather made, and harsher.

"Another, please," he said, the fiery liquid easing down his insides.

She slid him another shot, Buford Tee ingesting it with the same fervor as the first.

"You from 'round here?" Buford Tee asked.

Miss Carmelia said nothing.

"Uh...I said, you from 'round here?" Buford Tee repeated, thinking she had not heard him over the hum of the music playing in the joint.

"I heard you the first time," Miss Carmelia said, her pungent voice like butter to Buford Tee's ears.

Buford waited for a reply.

"You trying to pick me up?" she asked with directness.

"Well, uh, I...," Buford Tee fumbled.

"Mister, I'm gone tell you like it is," Miss Carmelia said bluntly, leaning forward and pointing toward the entrance of the joint. See that fella over there. That big, black husky nigger over there? He been trained to tell my ex-husband about every man that grin in my face. And my ex-husband. He crazy. He'll make it his business to hunt down that man and blow his brains out. So I suggest you order what you want to drink and take it back to your friend over there, whose looking like he's gone have a conniption because you trying to test some waters that done ran dry."

Buford Tee didn't know what to say. He ordered another shot of whiskey, paid for all he had drunk, and took his drink back to his seat.

"What happened?" Ton Stone asked, worriedly looking at the bouncer who was staring at Buford Tee. "What? What?"

"She said to come back later when old bulldog over there won't be around," Buford Tee lied, gulping down the whiskey to mask his bruised pride.

Her ex-husband entered the joint, the bouncer whispering something in his ear. He looked over at Buford Tee and, with swiftness, headed to the bar where Miss Carmelia was waiting.

Buford Tee and Ton Stone watched his every move, his black skin engulfing him.

"Uh oh," Ton Stone said. "I think you done done it now."

Her ex-husband grabbed Miss Carmelia by the arm and shoved her out back of the barrelhouse. Buford Tee stood to follow, but Ton Stone grabbed his arm and nodded toward the bouncer who was heading his way. Buford Tee sat back down and waited. Waited to see what her ex-husband needed with her out back.

"Man, you know how to find trouble, don't you?" Ton Stone said nervously.

"Ain't much fun if I don't go looking for it," Buford Tee said, a little concerned about Miss Carmelia.

It was a long while before her ex-husband came back inside. Buford Tee wondered where Miss Carmelia was but didn't dare go looking for her, especially with the black giant looming in the corner, prepared to stomp him down if he made a move on her.

Before anyone could make a move, the front door of the joint came crashing down, two burly, white officers rushing in with rifles pointed at all the patrons. Within seconds of the invasion, the back door was caved in, two more white officers racing in with rifles and pistols aimed at the startled crowd.

"Oh, shit," Ton Stone said. "Just what we needed."

"Everybody to the wall!" the lead officer shouted. "Get your face to the wall, I said, dammit. Right now!"

Intoxicated men and women jumped up and pressed their sweat-soaked, fully inebriated bodies against the wall, some using the wall as a respite from their intoxication, others, their highs blown by the invasion into the one place they felt was their own.

Buford Tee and Ton Stone followed suit, not wanting any trouble, particularly, Ton Stone, who was one day from leaving this hell hole called the South.

The ex-husband, who had been raided on a regular basis, had grown tired of the shake downs from the corrupt officers. He had paid a pretty penny to them to keep them at bay, but it seemed only to fuel the fire, their demanding more money each time they raided his establishment and to exert more control over him with each unwanted visit.

"What the hell is this?" he shouted.

"Now, Hawk, you know the drill," the lead officer said. "Cough it up, or your patrons going down to the jailhouse."

Hawk shook his head, gritting his teeth and cursing the lead officer under his breath, and then headed to the bar where he stashed the evening's till, pulling out a wad of cash and giving it to the lead officer, who didn't even count it.

"Two hundred. Hum. Good work, Hawk. Next week, make it three," he said, pointing to the newest officer. "Got another one on the payroll, you know."

The officers started backing out of the joint, their guns still pointed at the patrons, and particularly at Hawk. The lead officer was the last to depart, eyeing Miss Carmelia who had just entered the joint, her face red and bruised on the left side.

"I see you can't control that temper of yours again, Hawk," the lead officer said mockingly.

Hawk turned to see Miss Carmelia standing at the counter.

"Such a pretty face. Too bad she's a colored whore," the lead officer sneered.

With that last comment, Hawk pulled a knife from his back pocket, flicked it open, and tossed it with magnified force at the lead officer who had simultaneously lifted his shotgun and fired, the bullet tearing into Hawk's chest, the force of which propelled him backward into the bar, knocking it over and pinning Miss Carmelia under it. The bouncer pulled his gun to shoot the lead officer, but it was unneeded, the knife slicing into his right eye, paralyzing his body which seemed to take a moment to collapse. The other officers rushed back inside to see what happened, the bouncer throwing his gun under a table.

"What the hell happened here?" another officer yelled.

"Deputy Avery shot Hawk," the bouncer said. "And Hawk killed him dead."

Like chickens with their heads wrung off, the deputies ran around joint trying to act tough, harassing the patrons who repeatedly said the same phrase, "I ain't seen nothing, sir. My face was in the wall."

Frustrated, the deputies left the colored patrons to tend to Hawk's body. Two of the officers dragged Deputy Avery's body out of the joint and placed it in the squad car. The bouncer ran to Hawk to see if he was for sure dead. He was. Buford Tee and Ton Stone raced over to help Miss Carmelia, who was trapped under the collapsed bar. They pulled the structure from atop her and helped her to her feet.

"You alright?" Buford Tee asked.

"Yeah, I'm alright. I can't say the same for him," she said coldly, looking down at Hawk, a large pool of blood forming under his body.

Miss Carmelia leaned down and checked Hawk's pulse to see for herself if he was dead. She held her position for a moment, almost as if giving a short prayer. Then she stood abruptly.

"Get him up and put him in the wagon and take him to my house," she said with no emotion in her voice.

The bouncer and another hired hand lifted Hawk's body and hauled it outside to the wagon.

"Alright, y'all. Ain't nothing else to see here, so go home," Miss Carmelia said, heading to the back of the joint and returning with a pan of water.

"You okay?" Buford Tee asked. "Is there anything I can do?"

"You can leave," Miss Carmelia said frankly, squatting on the floor and dousing the blood-stained floor with water, the crimson-colored blood turning a pale pink.

Respecting her wishes, Buford Tee and Ton Stone walked slowly out of the joint.

"She don't need to be alone like this," Buford Tee told Ton Stone when they got outside to head home.

"Man, you don't give up, do you?" Ton Stone said. "Didn't I tell you that woman's trouble?"

"Well, ain't her trouble gone now?" Buford Tee asked, watching from outside as she wiped up all traces of blood from the floor.

"You don't even know the woman. And she didn't act like she was the least bit interested in you," Ton Stone said, smirking.

"She will be. Just give me time," Buford Tee said confidently. "Just give me time."

ROCK

The year the United States entered the War, Buford Tee Jefferson opened the Nickel and Dimer in Jones County. He purchased a run-down piece of property, located near the route of the New Orleans and Northeastern Railroad to build his juke joint. He wanted to attract the colored railroad workers and saw mill employees who had money to spend. It was a place the coloreds in Jones County could go that would be free of the raucousness and bawdiness of the barrelhouse crowd at the Hankering in Wayne County, a place to let off some steam without having to trudge twenty or more miles to the Hankering.

Buford Tee offered his prime whiskey at the Nickel and Dimer and hired local colored talent to perform for the patrons. Those that wanted a little more action could make their way to the Hankering, freely doling out money on the crib girls for their services, the crib girls happily obliging.

A year later the Eighteenth Amendment was passed, prohibiting the manufacture and sale of alcohol. It was now the law of the land, but it proved difficult to enforce. The Volstead Act solved this problem. When people in the county heard that everything from whiskey to rum to beer was being banned, they vehemently protested against the law, chiding that it violated their civil rights and infringed upon their personal liberties. If they wanted to drink, they felt it was their God-given right to do so. They also argued that if they could die for the country in the War, then they damn sure should have the right to take a drink whenever the notion hit them.

August thought the new law was going to put a dent in his whiskey-making business, but it actually gave it a boost, many residents stocking up on liquor just in case the ban would render the county completely dry. The sheriff of Jones County, Sheriff Coffield, never enforced the laws banning alcohol in his county, allowing August to continue his enterprise without interference.

As soldiers returned home from the War, they were surprised to learn that alcohol was banned in the States. They were angry, particularly, because alcohol was sold unreservedly overseas and they could indulge freely while on their tour of duty. The soldiers couldn't believe the evangelists and prohibitionists, that they had risked their lives for, had taken away a freedom they believed was guaranteed by the Constitution, something that helped them keep their sanity during the War, many coming home from the War addicted to the intoxicating brew.

Many colored soldiers made their way.to the Nickel and Dimer, dressed in their military uniforms, to knock back a few bottles of whiskey, tell some war stories, and gamble. The crowd welcomed the soldiers like they were colored celebrities. One soldier, in particular, Hezekiah Bennett, nicknamed Rock in the War because he had a head shaped like a rock, all lumpy and dented, bragged about how he saved a whole white infantry unit, telling the story with zeal, other soldiers refusing to recant their war stories, wanting only to forget the whole experience, the nightmares and flashbacks paralyzing them to the point they couldn't acclimate themselves back into society.

"At daybreak, you see, we were starting our advancement," Rock narrated, holding a whiskey bottle in one hand and a soldier's smoke in the other.

"Yeah, and what happened then?" one patron asked, listening intently to his tale.

"The enemy forces were closing in, you see," Rock added.

"Uh huh, uh huh," another patron said, urging Rock on, who had paused to take a swig of whiskey and a long drag on his Camel cigarette.

"There were men all over, see?" Rock continued. "Men laying out, some wounded, some dead."

"Go 'head," the first patron insisted, tired of his slow progress in the story.

"We couldn't stop. We had to leave the wounded," Rock said.

"Why?" the other patron asked.

"There was gunfire and shells all over our heads," Rock said. "We couldn't stop advancing until we got to a position to take the enemy out."

"And what happened then?" the first patron asked.

"Two white soldiers and me, we saw a shell hole and made a run for it," he replied.

"Yeah, uh huh," the other patron said, hanging on to Rock's every word.

"I managed to dive in," Rock said.

"Yeah?" the other patron said.

"They fell in after me," Rock added. "They was hit, both of them."

"And," the first patron egged on.

"I bandaged their wounds and got them stable," Rock said. "One guy lost his life. The other lost just his hand. Then I advanced forward. I had to leave them and take out the enemy."

"Did you take them out?" the other patron asked.

"Hell yeah, I took them out," Rock boasted. "We pushed them damn Germans back. We beat they asses. They gave us medals and welcomed us back to D.C. Colored soldiers, a colored platoon did that."

"Damn, you the man," the first patron commented. "You the damn man. Barkeep, get this soldier another drink!"

As more patrons entered the joint, they gathered around to hear Rock retell his story many times that night, each retell embellished a little bit more with exaggerated details. Rock didn't see any harm in it. He was a hero in their eyes, no doubt.

As the night went on, the soldiers also longed to feel a warm body next to them, keeping the local, single, colored ladies who were looking for a husband or a sugar papa busy on the dance floor. Those, not trying to be tied down to one woman, who wanted to just get laid would head to the Hankering to indulge themselves in the crib girls.

Rock and a few other colored soldiers entered the Hankering, again Rock retelling his war story to interested patrons. They would buy him drink after drink to keep his narrative going. The other soldiers, not interested in talking about the war, their memories more demoralizing than Rock's, would find a crib girl to entertain them, heading to the back rooms to get gratification. By three in the morning, the soldiers would have their fill of liquor and women and would be ready to head home, proudly wearing their uniforms that had become disheveled and soiled with sweat, alcohol, and sex.

Several admiring patrons offered to take Rock home. He turned them down, deciding, instead, to walk home since it was only a couple of miles away heading through town. He had hiked hundreds of miles in France, so that little jaunt was nothing for him.

When he reached town, he passed two white soldiers coming out of the Wayfarer's Lounge, a honky tonk for whites. Rock recognized one of the soldiers, the one missing his left hand, and rushed up to him to see how he was doing.

"Hey, remember me? In that shell hole in France?" Rock asked excitedly, believing the man would recognize him.

"What? Naw, I don't know you!" the soldier snapped.

"But remember? I pulled you out of that sniper fire. I bandaged you up. I saved your life," Rock continued, trying to jog the soldier's memory.

"Look, nigger. I told you I didn't know you. You ain't saved my ass. So get the hell out of my face!" the soldier said harshly.

Rock, puzzled by the soldier's angry display, fell silent. He was certain that was the man he had pulled from the gunfire.

"Sorry," Rock said and turned and walked away.

While walking home, Rock replayed the incident in his mind over and over, thinking the War had forged a common bond among all men in uniform, coloreds and whites. Apparently, it had not, based on that soldier's reaction. Still, Rock was positive that was the man whose life he had saved.

It was night, the air was thick and humid, and the sky was lit by gunfire. Rock and his colored platoon were advancing forward toward the Germans. The white platoons ahead of them had been hit from overhead by German Hun planes, spraying liquid fire at them. When they saw the planes coming their way, Rock and his platoon fell to the ground, the wind from the planes stirring up around their faces and cooling them off. They waited until the barrage ended and advanced forward once again, coming upon several wounded soldiers from the white platoon.

Rock could hear the Huns returning, and he knew he needed to get the wounded out of harm's way before the barrage of shrapnel and machine guns started pumping again. Rock pulled two white soldiers to a shell hole and helped to bandage them up. One soldier died, but the other, he was able to save his life, although he would lose his hand, blown off by shrapnel flying through the air. After Rock finished tying a tourniquet around the soldier's arm and bandaging his hand to stop the bleeding, he prepared to head to next pile of human bodies ahead of him, but the soldier grabbed his hand and thanked him for saving his life, his pale skin darkened by mud and blood covering his face and body. Rock nodded, the white man's face burned into his memory. Rock had not allowed himself to feel anything during his stint in the war, trying only to do his duty and make it back home alive. The look in the man's eyes almost made him cry, but he couldn't allow the tears to form, emotions a deadly weapon in a war. Rock told him he'd be okay and moved on to the bodies lying ahead of him.

Rock was less than a mile from home when he heard footsteps running behind him. He turned to see the two white soldiers barreling toward him. He took off running, but they overtook him and knocked him to the ground, punching and kicking him.

"You sumbabitch!" the handless soldier shouted.

"You ain't shit," the other soldier yelled. "You ain't nothing but a piece of trash, nigger."

"Done got high and mighty walking 'round here with that uniform on," the handless soldier snapped.

The other soldier beat Rock almost unconscious, and then he started ripping the uniform from Rock's body, hollering, "Take that damned uniform off. Disgracing our country."

When they finished with Rock, they left him nearly naked on the side of the dirt road. Rock didn't regain consciousness until early that morning. He was groggy and sore, his side throbbing. He sat up, giving his body some time to adjust to the pains shooting through him. Then he shook his head and tried to stand up, his legs stiffened by the cool, damp air. He looked around to see his clothes torn and strewn in the road. The tee shirt and underwear he had on were torn, and he wondered what had happened to him.

Rock stood up slowly, gaining his balance, and headed down the road, walking as close to the bushes as he could. After a short ways, he heard a car heading his way. He ducked behind some bushes and waited for the car to pass, but it didn't. It stopped on the side of the road. It was Buford Tee. He had seen the torn uniform in the road and wondered what happened, thinking the worse had occurred, another lynching.

"Shit. Shit. Shit," Buford Tee cursed.

The soldier, recognizing Buford Tee from the Nickel and Dimer, stepped out from behind the bushes and walked slowly toward him. Buford Tee looked up to see the half-naked man walking toward him, stunned but relieved at what he saw.

"Hey, you alright there?" Buford Tee asked.

"As much as I can be," Rock replied. "You mind sir, giving me a lift?"

"Sure," Buford Tee said, helping him to the car.

"You need a doctor?" Buford Tee asked, prepared to take him to one.

"No," Rock replied.

"You want me to take you home?" Buford Tee asked.

"Ain't got no home," Rock said, his parents having died a few years before he left for the War, Rock figuring joining up would give him a better chance at a good life.

"Where you been staying since you got home from the War?" Buford Tee asked.

"Wherever somebody would let me," Rock answered.

"Oh," Buford Tee said, noticing Rock was tired of answering questions and drifting in and out of consciousness.

Buford Tee took him to his house and helped him to a guest bedroom to let him recuperate. He called the colored county doctor to come see about him. The doctor gave him some pain medicine and told Buford Tee he'd be alright in a few days, no broken bones to keep him down. Buford Tee thanked the doctor and paid him for his services. When Rock awoke later that day, Buford Tee fried some catfish and cornbread for him and poured him a tall glass of whiskey.

"What happened to you, man?" Buford Tee asked, placing a tray in front of him.

The soldier told him what happened, not with the same exuberance he had been telling his war stories the night before at the Nickel and Dimer and at the Hankering.

"That's some shit," Buford Tee snapped. "A colored man risk his damn life in the War fighting for people that'll thank you when they scared shitless they gone die but act like you a piece of shit when they get back to the states."

"I know that was the man I saved," Rock said, still trying to convince himself of that truth.

It took a week for Rock to fully recover, Buford Tee allowing him to stay with him until he was well enough to get out on his own. Rock didn't have a job or a place to stay, so Buford Tee offered him a job at the Nickel and Dimer and set him up in a rental apartment he owned to help him get back on his feet.

THE HOUSE DOWN THE DIRT LANE

The first time I knew I needed to be scared of Furvis was the summer of 1960 in the early afternoon when he came down the dirt lane wielding a shotgun and shouting into the air. It was in the middle of July in the hottest part of the day, the temperature a scorching ninety-eight degrees. We had just finished hanging a barn of tobacco that morning and had stopped for lunch. Papa was fixing on his John Deere tractor while we were playing hopscotch and shooting marbles in the white sand of our front yard.

Papa noticed Furvis first, seeing him from a distance, his figure distorted by the hazy summer rays as he headed toward our house.

"Y'all chillen, git up and go in the house," Papa warned in a non-histrionic voice, trying not to alarm us.

"Why, Papa?" we asked, not having seen Furvis and not wanting to disrupt our game-playing. I was winning, so I definitely didn't want to go inside before claiming victory.

"Go on in the house, I said," he ordered with more emphasis on his words this time.

We didn't understand why he was interrupting our play and ordering us into the house, but we didn't question him a second time. We knew procrastinating when he told us to do something in that voice meant the next time he would have to say something to us, we'd get the belt taken to our hides.

We got up and headed toward the house, and before we got inside, Papa was calling for Mama to come to the door.

"Git my shotgun," he told Mama, who started to question him but saw Furvis moving closer to our home.

Concerned, she hurried us inside and returned to the back door in a rush to give Papa his shotgun, used only to kill hogs and to hunt cottontails and deer in the fall of the year.

"Git dem kids in the house and keep 'em there," he cautioned her, knowing we were the types to be warned of danger and still go running headlong right into it.

She pushed us into the kitchen and told us to get over in the corner while she stood guard at the kitchen window, watching worriedly as Furvis made his way into our backyard.

"Furvis, what you comin' up in my yard with that gun fo'?" Papa asked sternly, cocking his shotgun and aiming it toward Furvis.

Furvis slowed his gait but still waved his shotgun wildly, shouting aimlessly toward the sky.

"Furvis!" Papa shouted, lifting his shotgun and aiming it directly at Furvis.

Mama had made her way to the back door by now, turning back one last time to shush us and demanding we stay quiet. And hidden. She didn't want to take any chances with Furvis, so she picked up Papa's other shotgun, kept in the corner behind the washing machine, the one she vowed never to touch. Guns scared Mama, but at the moment, all that fear had rushed out of her, and she stood at the back door, the screened door propped open, with the shotgun cocked and aimed at Furvis. She had never touched a gun before let alone shot one, but she was as determined as any soldier in a war to defend her home front.

Furvis hadn't given Papa any problems in the years he had lived in the house down the dirt lane from us. Well, you really can't call what he lived in a house. It was a worn down, dilapidated shell of a house. It should have been condemned years ago, but when Furvis came around a few years after the Korean War looking for work, Papa helped him out, giving him a job as a farm hand and allowing him to live in the house if he was willing to do the handy work on it. Furvis agreed, but no handy work had ever been done on the house in all the years he lived there.

Furvis lived alone, and apparently wanted it that way. We never saw anyone go down the lane to visit him. And if you walked past his house, you could see him sitting on the porch in the shadows rocking slowly, back and forth, in his chipped metal slider, holding his shotgun on his lap. Papa had to tell Furvis on many occasions to put that shotgun up when we had to go down the lane past his house to crop tobacco.

"If one of my chillen git hurt 'cause of that gun, I'm gone kill ya," Papa told him the first time my brother came running home scared shitless. And I mean shitless. He had shitted in his pants because he believed Furvis was going to shoot him. We thought it was really funny, but Papa didn't. Papa knew Furvis wasn't all right in the head. And he was subject to go off on a shooting rampage at any given time, provoked by almost anything. So Papa warned him as long as he lived on his property, none of his kids had better get hurt because of his shotgun.

Apparently, Furvis believed Papa would kill him. If he didn't, we certainly did. Although we could never imagine Papa shooting anybody. I believed he would have shot Furvis if something were to happen to any of his kids.

"Furvis, I ain't tellin' you agin; git outta my yard with dat gun. I ain't got no beef with you," Papa warned again, still holding the shotgun aimed at Furvis. By now Papa had eased behind his tractor for protection, in case Furvis got foolish.

Furvis paused, searching the sky for something. He stared fiercely to the East and then turned the shotgun up toward the air, and in a flash, a shot went off, startling Papa who had his shotgun cocked and was prepared to fire at Furvis.

Stunned, Furvis dropped to the ground and scurried toward the barn, pressing his back against the cool metal siding, shouting, "In-coming! Lock and load!"

Papa didn't know what had happened at first. He didn't see Furvis fire his shotgun. And he knew he did fire his own. Then he turned back to see Mama standing in the back door with the screened door propped open and the shotgun in her hands, cocked again and ready to be fired again if it was called for.

Surprised at Mama, and a little impressed, Papa allowed an impish grin to ease across his face. Knowing she was pulling up the ranks, Papa steadied his shotgun back on Furvis in case he tried to fire at him. Or Mama.

Furvis sat on the ground, clutching his shotgun like it would somehow shield him from his enemy, his faced draped in fear and his body shaking uncontrollably.

"Furvis, throw yo' shotgun o'er here," Papa shouted. "I ain't givin' you but one warnin'."

"You see 'em? They comin' fo' us! They up dar. They comin' fo' us! You see 'em?" Furvis shouted, pointing up towards the sky.

"Naw, I don't see nothin', Furvis. Ain't nothin' up dar. Ain't nothin' up dar, Furvis!" Papa shouted.

Furvis seemed disoriented, like he didn't know where he was or how he had gotten there. Papa said Furvis got like that sometimes. Thinking he was still in the War and seeing those fighter planes flying overhead.

Furvis started to mumble to himself, "One thousand eight days, four hours and forty-three minutes. One thousand eight days, four hours and forty-three minutes." Repeating the length of his stint in the War several times before he slid the shotgun across the ground toward Papa.

Papa made his way around the tractor, picking up the shotgun, and standing before Furvis.

"You need to git on back home," Papa said calmly, yet firmly. "I won't need you fo' the rest of the day."

Furvis didn't seem to hear Papa, but he got up slowly, still mumbling, "One thousand eight days, four hours and forty-three minutes," and stammering back down the dirt lane toward his house.

Papa, a little shaken, but nonetheless relieved, turned to see Mama still pointing the shotgun at the vacant space where Furvis once stood, making sure he did not return. When she saw him halfway down the dirt lane to his house, she lowered the shotgun and breathed a sigh of relief.

"I didn't know you knew how to shoot that thang," Papa teased, walking toward Mama, knowing she had never touched any of his shotguns before.

"Here, take this thang. Ugh!" Mama said passing the shotgun to Papa and wringing her hands as if some kind of poison had rubbed off on them.

Papa chuckled as Mama turned and headed into the house to check on us—we were still huddled in the corner.

THE FIELD WORKER

That morning, in late June 1964, in Tupelo, Mississippi, volunteer field workers were going door to door in the black neighborhoods to help initiate voter registration drives and to build community relations. A young white field worker walked through her neighborhood with three other black field workers. Hers was the first house on their list. He paused in front of a pale green, tin-roofed house, the paint peeling in places all over the house. The porch was rickety and sagged as he stepped up on it.

He knocked on her door, and her eight-year-old son answered, saying "Mama, da 'surance man's y'ere." The only white people her son had ever seen at their front door were insurance agents, coming to collect premiums.

She was in the midst of preparing breakfast before heading off to work downtown at the cotton mill. Interrupted and irritated, she went to the door, her hair in rollers and a scarf and a laced apron tied around her full figure, asking haughtily, "Wat d'ya want?"

The field worker, a young, energetic, college student from Queens College in New York, said in a northern accent, "Ma'am, I'm not an insurance man. I'm here to help get you registered to vote."

She looked him up and down and leaned her head out of the door, looking to her left and her right, and then she closed the door in his face. Her son was perplexed as to why the young white boy was in his neighborhood. The only other white person he'd ever seen that came through their neighborhood was the sheriff coming to arrest someone. Her son pulled back the curtain to see the field worker make his way to the next house on the block, knocking on the door and waiting for someone to answer.

She told her son, "Git away fum dat window 'fore somebody be shot at ya, boy."

"But Ma," he moaned.

"Do wat I said," she ordered and went back to her kitchen to finish preparing breakfast.

Her son released the curtain reluctantly and went to his bedroom.

"Vota reg'stration, humph," she grumbled to herself as she flipped two fried eggs in the hot skillet.

For as long as she could remember, nobody she knew in her small neighborhood had ever managed to get registered to vote, and it got to a point where it was futile to even try. She remembered the poll taxes her papa had to pay just for the right to vote in local elections. The first time her papa went to register to vote, the county clerk told him he would have to pass a literacy test. He couldn't, of course, at that time as he had only limited literacy skills, but he was determined to pass it. And pass it he did, with the help of a local colored schoolteacher who taught him to read and write. She also taught him the constitution and how to answer questions on the literacy tests. This occurred for three months straight after working long hours at the saw mill. She remembered on a few occasions over the years when her papa, making his way to the courthouse to vote, was met with violence from several of the white locals, including the sheriff, who stood back and allowed him to be attacked and did nothing to stop it.

She remembered these things.

The following day, the same young field worker returned to her door at the same time as the previous day. Her son once again answered the door. "Mama, dat votin' man's back agin," he yelled to the kitchen where she was cooking a pot of grits and sausage patties.

"Damn," she hollered from the kitchen, the hot grits spitting and popping her on the arm.

She emerged from the kitchen with a scowl on her face. "Wat d'ya want now?" she snapped, wiping her hands and arms in a dishtowel.

"Ma'am, I want to give you this voter registration form and ask that you join the Freedom Party," he said quickly, passing the form to her and stepping inside her door.

"Freed'm Party?" she said, taking the form and glancing at it with noninterest. "Wat's dat?"

"Oh, Ma'am," he said excitedly, thinking he had garnered her attention to the cause and wanted desperately to explain its purpose and hopefully get her to sign up. "It's an organization to help get people registered to vote. You see, many people in Mississippi have been denied the right to vote, and we, the SNCC, the Student Nonviolent Coordinating Committee, are helping to spread the word."

She paused as if pondering all he had just said.

"Would you like to sign up?" he asked hopefully.

She mulled over the form for a moment and then said, "Dat all sounds great'n all, but naw," walking toward the door and escorting him out, again closing the door in his face.

She threw the form on the coffee table and headed back to her kitchen to resume her cooking. Her son picked up the form and read what he could make out. The lady down the street from them was a school teacher and spent many afternoons teaching the black children in the neighborhood to read. Her son was one of those children.

"Mama, ya goin' join the Freed'm Party?" he asked, following her into the kitchen and showing her the form.

"Don't botha me wit' dat mess," she said angrily. "All dat rhet'ric ain't goin' change nothin'."

Her son took the form back into the front room and sat down on the sofa studying it. The field worker made his way to the next house. He had been to that house before and had left a form for the owner to fill out. He knocked on her door, and when the lady opened it, he asked if she had filled out the form. She said no. And that she wouldn't fill it out.

"May I ask why, Ma'am?" he said pitifully, feeling like no one was understanding the importance of the cause. *Didn't they want change--he thought. Didn't they believe change could and would happen?* He was still hopeful, thinking the next time he came by, she would be ready to sign up. He wasn't going to give up. No, he wouldn't give up.

"Naw, you may not," she said in a fearful tone, "and please don't come back 'round y'ere no mo'," slamming the door in his face.

Cursing under his breath and feeling dejected, he returned to the awaiting car where two other field workers, both black, had been waiting for him with similar results. They got that all the time. If a person didn't sign up within the first five minutes, they wouldn't, no matter how long the field workers talked with them and tried to explain why they should join the Freedom Party. It boiled down to fear. Understandable fear that many of the northern white field workers had not experienced first-hand on their short stints in Mississippi that summer. Even though they were met with constant rejections, they refused to give up, telling every one of the inhabitants they would be back.

For three days, she had not heard from nor seen the field worker. In fact, no one in that neighborhood had seen any of the field workers. They had been told to lay low for a few days because they had received word of the disappearance of three other volunteer field workers.

The significance of the project had not hit the young field worker until then, after hearing about the three volunteers. He remembered back in Ohio, the night before he was to start his expedition into Mississippi, he was briefed on what to expect down there in the Delta.

"Expect death," the SNCC leader warned. "Expect to die. And if you get jailed, go quietly. Don't try to talk your way out of nothing. That's what the $500 you are to bring along is for. To bail you out."

When he heard these words "expect death," he didn't really think he'd be risking his life. He didn't believe people could harbor such hatred towards their fellow man that they would harm them, or even kill them. There were laws in place to prevent this kind of thing. He thought they were only telling them that so that they would be more diligent in doing the job, not that they were literally putting their lives at risk.

The next evening, the young field worker saw her son playing marbles with a group of children, some in tattered clothing, some barefoot and unclean, outside in the yard. They were seated on the ground in a circle surrounding a hand full of marbles. He stood nearby watching them play. It was as if they had no cares in the world, unaware of the layers of anger, resentment, cynicism, and discontent among black Mississippians toward the white Mississippi establishment, unaware of the brutality of Mississippi racism and how it had infected the people of that state, unaware of the volatile emotional cross-currents that ran through all of them, both black and white. These children seemed totally unaffected, the wonderful cheerfulness of their squeals and laughter permeating the humid summer air. The image of their carefree play almost brought him tears.

"Hey son," he said.

"Hey mista," her son replied, not halting his play.

"Is your mother home?" he asked.

"Uh hum," the son answered, not allowing himself to be distracted from his turn at shooting marbles. He knuckled down and shot his shooter, winning that round of the game.

"Do you mind going to get her?" he asked holding his stomach, his balance unsteady.

He jumped up and ran inside and returned a few moments later. His mother followed slowly and stopped in the doorway.

"Tony, whatcha callin' me for, boy?" she shouted, startling the field worker, who lost his balance and fell over her steps, voter registration papers flying out of his hands, the children snickering at his misfortune.

"Oh, iz you agin," she said, recognizing him from a few days earlier.

"Yes Ma'am," he said, trying to get up.

"You gotta be careful 'round y'ere. I ain't got no money to be payin' for nobody dat cain't watch were dey steppin'," she said angrily, pushing open the screened door.

"Ma, he bleedin'," Tony said, noticing blood trickling down his arm.

"He couldn't of hurt hisself dat bad fallin' off some steps," she said, stepping outside on the steps to inspect him. Then she noticed the bleeding, which softened her hard-bitten demeanor towards him.

"Help me git him in da house," she said, stepping down and taking him by one arm and her son taking him by the other.

The other children picked up the forms and followed behind them, curious about this man that kept appearing at their houses. Inside, they helped him to her sofa.

"Take dem kids in the back and stay dar 'til I call ya," she said.

"Aw, Ma," Tony lamented.

"Go 'head now," she ordered.

She disappeared into the kitchen to get a cloth and some liniment to clean his wound. The field worker heard a television playing in another room and saw two children that were not outside, both younger than her son, wander out, staring at him with their bright, beautiful eyes. He smiled at them. They smiled back bashfully, standing by their bedroom, a safe distance from him, although they were intrigued by him. In his few weeks of canvassing the black neighborhoods, he discovered that the black children—although many not fearful of him—were well aware that he was not like them. Even at a very young age, they were well aware of his difference—his color.

Curious, Tony came out of his room and sat down on the floor, cross legged, next to the field worker, holding the forms in his hands. "Wat's a Freed'm Party?" he asked.

For a moment, the field worker couldn't respond. He had almost given up on the project, after running into a violent mob down at the courthouse earlier. When he started out, he wanted to be a part of something that could radically change the South and America as a whole. But the few weeks he had been out in the field, being turned away by the multitudes of blacks too afraid to become involved and witnessing first-hand the severe state of oppression in Mississippi, almost caused him to lose his resolve.

He, like the many other white volunteers, came from privileged backgrounds and had experienced few limits imposed on him by race or class. Having lived in an all-white, middle-class neighborhood in the North all of his life and having limited exposure to racial diversity, the field worker did not realize the level of racism that had pervaded Mississippi and the problems associated with it.

And now he was there, in the thick of it, wise enough to be fearful for his well-being, but too naïve not to believe that his sacrifice would affect the major changes the project envisioned. And the interest of her son in something he did not understand but was willing to learn about renewed in him that desire to help bring about those changes.

"The Freedom Party," he started, scratching his head, thinking how to explain what he was soliciting in a language a child could understand. "Well, the Mississippi Freedom Democratic Party, that's the official name."

He paused, not noticing his mother standing in the doorway of the kitchen holding a bottle of liniment and a clean cloth.

"See, Mississippi, the way it is now, won't allow blacks to vote," he continued. "The Freedom Party is protesting this long held rule, and people like me are helping to spread the word. We are trying to give people who were denied that right an opportunity to vote in this November's election. We are signing up party supporters at their homes so they won't have to go to the county courthouse to register to vote. They won't have to face violent opposition, or be fearful of losing their jobs, or have to take unfair literacy tests. The Freedom Party wants to change the way things have been done in Mississippi for decades and treat every citizen, particularly the black citizens, fairly. We are going to send delegates to the national Democratic Party Convention in August to represent the disenfranchised voices of Mississippi."

"You white, ain't ya?" the boy asked in a serious tone, studying the field worker's features carefully, almost as if trying to figure out what was so different between them.

Startled, and a bit tickled, the field worker chuckled, "Uh, yes."

"Den wy come dem white folks don't want black folks ta vote?" the son asked straightforwardly, his solid assessment of the issue unsettling the field worker.

"'Cause dey don't want nothin' ta change down y'ere," his mother interrupted, startling the field worker, who turned quickly toward her.

"I'm sorry, Ma'am," he said nervously. "I was just...."

"I know wat ya waz just doin'," she said coolly. "And my son is nosey. Git on in dat back room. And take dem girls witcha."

"I'm sorry," he said again, worried that she was going to kick him out for involving her child in something that most of the grownups didn't want to be a part of themselves.

She walked toward him and sat on the sofa beside him. "Lit me see dat arm," she said gruffly.

She lifted it and inspected it, noticing a healed-over gash that had reopened in the fall. She dabbed a bit of liniment on the cloth, tapping it lightly on the wound. He flinched from the mild sting and then relaxed. She dabbed a bit more on the cloth and cleaned the wound well. He sat there, examining her round face and bright eyes, her demeanor now much unlike the first time when he came to her door. There was slight hint of a smile forming in the corner of her mouth as she cleansed his wound, her nurturing touch reminding him of his own mother.

When she finished tying a cloth around his arm, he said, "Thank you."

"Dey attacked ya, didn't dey?" she asked.

He paused, not wanting to give her more reasons to throw him out again.

"Word git 'round down y'ere. We heard 'bout dose beatin's at the courthouse yesterday. You was down dar won'tcha?" she said.

"Yes Ma'am," he said. "We were marching in protest, and a mob attacked us. I managed to get away."

"'Parently not 'fore gittin' ruffed up, huh?" she said.

102

"Yes Ma'am," he replied, a look of discouragement blanketing his face.

She stood up suddenly, taking the liniment and the cloth back into the kitchen. He waited a few minutes, thinking she would return momentarily. When she didn't, he didn't know what to make of her abrupt exit and decided not to push his luck with her. He picked up the voter registration forms, all but one, leaving it on the coffee table, and turned to head to the front door.

Just as he turned the doorknob, she called out to him, "Now tell me mo' 'bout dis Freed'm Party," returning with a plate of fried chicken, stewed cabbage, boiled potatoes, and a glass of excessively sweet iced tea.

Stunned, but pleasantly surprised, he closed the door back and returned to the sofa.

"Ya mus' be hungry," she said, passing the plate to him and sitting down beside him.

"Yes Ma'am," he said, taking a bite of the crispy chicken, thankful for her generosity. "I am."

She watched the frail young field worker take several more bites of the chicken and then wash it down with some tea.

"So were ya fum?" she asked curiously, a loose lock of his dark brown hair falling into his face.

"New York, Ma'am," he answered, his mouth filled with steamed cabbage.

"Hum," she pondered, propping her chin on her left hand and her elbow on her left knee and examining his lean frame. "I heard 'bout dem missin' volunteers."

The field worker nodded his head, acknowledging the fact.

"Mus' be a real fool ta come down y'ere to risk yo' life fo' a cause dat ain't even yo' own," she added, shaking her head slowly in disbelief, now observing him with a renewed sense of respect.

He swallowed the cabbage and took another swig of the sweetened tea and then smiled at the woman, at last feeling that he had somehow managed to gain her respect, if not her trust.

Still shaking her head, she picked up the form and said, "Now, back ta dis Freed'm Party."

Gladly, he began, "Well…."

AUNT LUELLA'S HOUSE

Like clockwork, every Saturday Papa went outside to the carport to warm up his 1969 AMC Rambler station wagon before heading to church. Bracing against the cold air, he got in the car hurriedly and turned the ignition, the car grinding and coughing until the engine roared. He pressed the emergency break and set the car to neutral and let it warm up, and then he headed back into the house.

"Maybelle, you and dem kids ready to go?" he shouted down the hallway to hurry us along.

Waiting impatiently by the pot-bellied stove, Papa knew Mama would be putting the finishing touches on her outfit for the Saturday service, her slim figure draped in a dark blue dress and a wide-brimmed church hat that showered her face in a sweeping canopy of shade. All the women in the church wore those wide-brimmed hats. Sometimes I think each service they tried to outdo the other women, wearing an even more boisterous hat, dressed in all manner of pins, ribbons, and birds—and flowers—roses, carnations, and forget-me-nots—and feathers—goose, ostrich, peacock, and pheasant. The more ostentatious the hat, the better.

When Mama didn't hear us stirring, she headed to our rooms to make sure we were dressed. Many weekends she'd find us still lying in beds, our hair unkempt, our faces unwashed, and our sleepy heads buried under the heavy quilted covers. And today was no different. She pulled back the multicolored, crazy quilts, heavy and hand-sewn, made of old clothing too small for us children and filled with old blankets, pants, and coats worn well beyond any use.

"Swish," the sound of a thin, freshly broken, flexible switch from the pear tree behind the house sliced the air and whipped my exposed legs.

"Ow!" I howled, being startled awake by the lashing.

"Didn't I tell y'all to get up and get dressed?" my mother said as she popped my two-year-old baby sister's legs lightly with her hands to awaken her.

Then she headed to my younger brother's room to switch him out of bed. To avoid their being late to church, we begged to stay home. We knew we weren't old enough to stay alone—my brother was eight, and I was ten—so we asked our older brothers who never wanted to look after us, and in actuality, my parents really didn't trust them to look after us. After all, they were boys with short attention spans and would just as soon leave us in the house alone, telling us to sit quietly in front of the black and white television while they went off with their friends to play stick ball or go fishing down by the rock quarry. Several times my parents would come home from church to find us in the kitchen attempting to cook some sliced and battered potatoes on the gas stove. Short of burning down the house, they feared we'd douse ourselves with the hot oil and end up in the hospital ward with third-degree burns like our cousin who died a few years earlier from pulling down a pot of hot cooking lard on top of her.

After my brothers refused to be our caretakers for the day, we asked, "What about Aunt Luella?"

"I guess we ain't got no choice now, do we?" Mama said. "Hurry up 'fore your Papa come down the hall with his belt."

We knew we didn't want that to happen. Papa was six foot four and as thick as a football running back. We ran to the bathroom and washed up as fast as we could and then got dressed in our Saturday play clothes.

Then we gobbled down some cheese grits and sausage patties Mama had cooked earlier, washing them down with some Tang, the zingy orange flavor lingering at the back of our tongues.

"Y'all come on," Papa urged as we all loaded into the warmed automobile.

For some unexplainable reason whenever we headed to church, I'd get this overwhelmingly nauseous feeling in the pit of my stomach. I always sat in back seat behind Papa, my baby sister in the middle, and my younger brother on the right. To pacify the squeamish feeling, I'd crack my window a bit. That always seemed to help until my baby sister would cry out she was cold.

"Roll that window back up," Papa would say, his baby girl always getting her way.

"You crybaby," I'd mumble to her, shooting an evil glare at her daring her to say another word.

It took about twenty minutes to get from our house to my Aunt Luella's house. She lived in the city limits on a side street in a shotgun house. Hers was the second house on the left of a long row of shotgun houses. Papa turned down the dirt lane, a cloud of dust rising up behind our car. It was always dusty down that lane. If you sat on the porch when someone's car came flying down the lane, you were sure to get a face full of dust and grit. The houses were so close to the dirt lane, you could reach out and touch the passing cars.

Since Papa was in a rush to get to church, he pulled in front of Aunt Luella's house and let Mama get out and escort us into the house. Mama greeted Aunt Luella who always seemed to be in a foul mood. That was just her disposition, but to the unfamiliar, she could be intimidating.

"You leaving dem brats here?" she asked harshly.

We were hoping she wasn't in too foul a mood that she would tell Mama she didn't want to be bothered. That happened occasionally whenever Uncle Levy was in town.

"You got something to do?" Mama asked.

"Naw, I guess not," she said nonchalantly.

"Thanks, Sis," Mama said, giving her a couple of jars of canned stewed tomatoes, her penance for leaving us with her.

No, Aunt Luella didn't mind us staying with her. She treated us like her personal maid servants, or more like her slaves, making us do all kinds of work around her house. She was going to get her day's worth of chores out of us before we went home. We knew Aunt Luella was a tyrant, but we felt staying with her was the lesser of two evils. Sitting in church from ten in the morning to almost five that evening practically killed us every Saturday and Sunday and sometimes Fridays at Association time, our attention spans not longer than the flutter of a hummingbird's wing. If we weren't hitting at each other behind Mama's back, we were squirming on the brick-hard wooden church benches, trying to work back the feeling in our behinds, which had grown numb, or we were swinging our legs over the side of the wooden benches, banging the backs of our heels against the benches, prompting Mama to reach over and quietly and undetectably pinch a plug out of our legs. We wouldn't dare cry out—that would cause her to take us out to the car with the windows rolled up and switch our behinds. We'd whimper and heave uncontrollably trying not to let out a wail that would bring the church service to a screeching halt. Embarrass Mama like that, and we were sure to get a good old-fashioned whipping with the belt from Papa when we got home. That we didn't want, so we would snivel in quiet. Sometimes a kindly Sister would ask what was wrong and offer us a piece of peppermint or butterscotch candy to soothe away our tears, but Mama would tell her we were alright, and she'd take the candy and put it in her purse until we could act right.

Aunt Luella would act lovingly towards us in front of Mama and Papa, saying kind words clean up until they turned the corner of the dirt lane and headed down Main Street to church. Then she'd tell us in no uncertain terms how rotten we were. That our mama spoiled us and how she wasn't going to put with the antics of some bratty ass kids. I must admit, we were a handful. We fought each other. We called each other out our names. We talked back to Aunt Luella. And we got smacked for it. After one or two times of getting swatted on the back of our heads for being mouthy, we learned to curse her under our breaths. Although it didn't have the same effect as talking back to her, it did bring us some satisfaction.

Aunt Luella was the way she was because when she and Uncle Levy were together, he stayed drunk all the time and could never stay away from Miss Velma's shot house. He claimed he was there only for the liquor, but Aunt Luella believed he was there seeing that loose woman. They had been on the outs for years, arguing and bickering and breaking up, getting back together and loving and being nice, and then breaking up again. A year ago he left Aunt Luella for good.

Every now and then they would see each other, usually around Christmas and on her birthday. Those were the times she was in a better mood. I wouldn't say the best mood because I don't think she had one. But she was more tolerable at those times than at any other.

Last Christmas Eve when Uncle Levy was expected to come by Aunt Luella's house, the day started out on a happy note, but by the end of the night, all hell had broken loose. My family had stopped by earlier in the day, a tradition we had done for as long as I could remember. Mama's mama had been sick for a long time. A stroke had kept her bedridden for the last few years. Aunt Luella took her in and cared for her. Or rather, Mama's kids cared for her. There were six of us kids still at home, our older siblings having moved out when they graduated high school. Aunt Luella made it clear to Mama that she needed to help out with Grandma, so Mama loaned us out, one of us a week to stay with Aunt Luella and help care for Grandma. We didn't mind because we loved Grandma, and we wanted to spend as much time with her as we could.

All our aunts and uncles made a point of coming home for Christmas, particularly to see Grandma and make that time of the year special for her. Anyone who didn't, better have had a good excuse, like death. Nothing short of that would satisfy Aunt Luella, who could make anyone feel guilty for not doing their fair share to make Grandma feel loved—loved according to Aunt Luella's standards. Aunt Luella's house would be full of family members from newborn babies to elderly and wise matriarchs. Most of the adults, and even some of the teenagers who thought they were grown, would be drinking during this time—the teenagers standing around the side of the house passing around a flask stolen from one of their parents for each of them to sneak a taste. Uncle Abe was notorious for bringing his White Lightning to add to homemade egg nog, and Cousin Ned always made a large batch of scuppernong wine and gave all the drinkers a Mason jar full of it. Mama and Papa didn't drink, so their share went to our Uncle Hank, who could drink anyone under the table.

When Uncle Levy arrived, the festivities truly began. He could turn a drab get-together into an all-night comedy show. All of the kids loved him because he liked to perform magic tricks for us, pulling quarters out of our ears and playing Three Card Monte, not for money though. Mama and Papa wouldn't let us gamble. There'd be a competition between the kids and the aunts and uncles to see who could get Uncle Levy to entertain them, he graciously agreeing to satisfy everyone. Except Aunt Luella, who always seemed to be in a foul mood whenever Uncle Levy took center stage in her house. She would retreat to the kitchen to take a swig of White Lightning from a flask she kept hidden behind a cabinet in the corner of the room. Mama and Papa knew what she was doing, but we kids never knew she drank like that. She would return a short while later and stand in the doorway leaning against the doorframe with a silly grin on her face while Uncle Levy entertained the crowded room, children and adults alike falling over from laughter, all of them clapping, cheering, and egging him on for more.

Uncle Levy could light up Aunt Luella's face the minute he walked through the door. Throughout the night when they thought no one was looking, they'd be huddled up in the corner of the room or pressed up against the kitchen sink, Uncle Levy whispering sweet nothings in her ear and nibbling on her neck, and Aunt Luella giggling like a schoolgirl with a crush on the star football player. It was sweet to see them like that. Why they couldn't stay that way, we all knew, but it was nice to see her in a better mood when Uncle Levy came around. But before the night was over, usually around midnight, Uncle Levy's unrestrained antics could bring out the worst side of her any of us children had ever seen.

"Levy," Aunt Luella snapped, his name rolling acidly off her tongue whenever one of our unmarried uncles' lady friends happened to accompany him to Aunt Luella's house. "Git yo' ass over h'yere!"

And the entertainment would come to a screeching halt.

"Baby...Baby, c'mon now," Uncle Levy would say, trying to assuage the ensuing anger raging inside her.

He knew she was jealous, and his shameless flirtations with any female non-relatives, and even any female relatives three times removed were all it took to set her off.

"Git out!" she'd shout, picking up anything handy to throw at him, everyone in her direct line of fire ducking to make sure not to be clobbered by a shoe, or a vase, or a telephone, whatever she could get her hands on. "Git out, raight now!"

And that would be the end of the entertainment for the evening. Aunt Luella would retreat to her bedroom while Uncle Levy made his rounds, saying his goodbyes to everyone, the children in particular disappointed that Aunt Luella had made him leave. We didn't understand what he had done to warrant that kind of backlash. We all secretly cursed her again under our breaths and out of ear shot of the grownups, mainly our parents. It wouldn't be long after he left that the rest of the family members would make excuses to leave early, and the house would be empty, except for Aunt Luella and Grandma, who had gone to bed hours earlier.

We wouldn't see Uncle Levy for months until Aunt Luella's birthday rolled around in June. Until then she'd be in a foul mood for months. Every time Uncle Levy came around to visit, however, something bad always seemed to happen to him. I don't know if he drew bad luck to himself, but it did seem to follow him like a dark cloud. Almost monthly, we'd hear rumors about him getting into some kind of trouble—a run-in with a jealous husband, an altercation with some ruffians he owed a gambling debt to, or his ducking and dodging the law for some petty offenses.

The second Saturday of June was Aunt Luella's birthday. My brother and I spent the day with her—although she refused to keep my baby sister because she would cry non-stop whenever Mama left her sight, and Aunt Luella was not about to be saddled with a whiney ass baby all day, so Mama and Papa took her to church with them. And because it was her birthday.

Aunt Luella pranced merrily around the house in anticipation of Uncle Levy's arrival. She made me and my little brother clean her house. I had the chores of washing the dishes, mopping the floors, and cleaning the bathroom. I hated cleaning up after somebody else, especially the bathtub. Ugh! My brother helped her move furniture so that she could sweep behind chairs and under beds, and he took out the trash. By early afternoon we were exhausted. She did allow us to take a nap, mainly to get us out of her hair while Uncle Levy visited. When we woke up, Uncle Levy still had not been by to see her. By then, she was getting irritated and made us go outside to play.

Aunt Luella's backyard was not that large, and it was a shared yard with the lady next door to her on the right, Miss Darcy. On the left there was a six-foot metal fence that separated her house from the lady on the left of her, Miss Mamie. Aunt Luella didn't like her. Mama said it was because they had the same taste in men. Namely Uncle Levy. The chain link fence was completely covered with dense, self-clinging Boston Ivy and ran the perimeter of both Aunt Luella's and Miss Darcy's backyard.

In the warm summer sun, my brother and I enjoyed exploring Aunt Luella's backyard. We played cops and robbers and cowboys and Indians—we always fought over who would get to be the Indian, and I usually won out. Then I ran around tapping my hand over my mouth to make the war hoop as we entered into a mock battle. I always won the battle because I was almost a head-length taller than my little brother and could easily take him down. When we tired of playing good guys and villains, we took one of Aunt Luella's Mason jars and hammered three holes in the cap to capture lightning bugs. We kept them in the jar for a while, watching their small bodies glow as we cupped our hands around the jar to block out the light.

Then hunger started to set in, so we sneaked down the dirt lane to Miss Margaret's Country Store and bought some penny candy. My brother had a sweet tooth and loved Tootsie Rolls and Moon Pies. I had less of a sweet obsession and desired anything salty like pretzels, potato chips, or peanuts. Whole dill pickles were my favorites, but they were five cents, so I didn't buy any of them. Then we gobbled down our booty so that there were no tell-tale signs of our leaving her backyard without permission. On a few occasions when Aunt Luella was preoccupied, we would manage to get back to her house before she realized we were gone, but the few times she did catch us leaving her backyard without telling her warranted a swat on the back of our heads and a punishment of going to bed in the middle of the day. Try falling to sleep when you are hyped up on a bag of penny candy. It can't be done. Then we'd get it again from Mama and Papa when they came to pick us up.

The back fence was covered with Boston ivy, but there were sections that exposed Main Street running directly behind Aunt Luella's house. It was a paved, two-way street cutting through the center of town. We were not allowed to go out of the yard at any time. If we followed the fence, it led to the stop sign at the end of the dirt lane Aunt Luella's house sat on. And to Main Street.

On many occasions we would sit at the exposed section of the fence watching the city dwellers making their way up and down Main Street. They couldn't see us, our small bodies shielded by the climbing, leafy vines, which was especially thrilling to my brother and me. We would pretend to be spies outwitting our unmatched adversaries, shooting them with invisible guns as they walked past our hiding spot. On those hot summer days, we could spend hours watching the goings-on on Main Street, the street cop directing traffic when the signal lights weren't working, the drunken wino that made his way up and down Main Street begging for some change to go to Miss Margaret's store to buy a bottle of Wild Irish Rose, the Jehovah Witnesses who walked door-to-door spreading their ministry and the *Watch Tower* and *Awake!* magazines to whoever would take them.

We were in the middle of our play when Aunt Luella shouted, "Git y'all asses in this house," startling us and bringing, once again, an end to our simple entertainment.

"We already cleaned her stinkin' house," my brother lamented under his breath.

Again we cursed her in silence. She made us come inside to shell black-eyed peas and shuck a bushel of corn for freezing, fruits of Mama and Papa's labor. We sat in the front room with all the windows raised to let in the cool summer breezes while Grandma monitored our handy work. We could see Aunt Luella through the opened window sitting on the front porch rocking in her pine green metal porch glider, the gentle winds undoing her finely coiffed hair she spent all morning having Miss Marcy fix up. Every now and then we'd see her get up and walk to the edge of the porch to look down the dirt lane for Uncle Levy. He still had not shown up, and her mood was growing more vinegary as the day went on.

After we finished our chores, we ate lunch and were allowed to go back outside to play. We stayed in the back yard trying our best to stay out of Aunt Luella's way for fear of being summoned, once again, to perform chores. We resumed our stakeout at the ivy-covered fence, but there were no interesting characters walking by to exact our revenge upon, so we decided to entertain ourselves in the alleyway between Aunt Luella's house and Miss Darcy's, a two-foot wide, narrow passageway that served as our secret tunnel into an imaginary world far, far away.

In the dimly lit passageway, we could hear the distant hum of a 1969 Cadillac DeVille Convertible turning down the dirt lane to Aunt Luella's house. We knew that hum. Aunt Luella knew it too. It was Uncle Levy's car, and its distinctive sound was music to her ears. We ran to the front of the house to await its arrival, but Aunt Luella ordered us to go back to playing. We obeyed reluctantly, walking back to our dimly lit passageway but not too far that we couldn't see Uncle Levy's dark red convertible. We stood there in silence, disappointed that we wouldn't get the chance to sit in the back seat of his car.

Aunt Luella stood on the porch waiting anxiously as the convertible made its slow arrival. She was already irritated with Uncle Levy for keeping her waiting all day, and now he seemed to be taking his own sweet time getting to her house. As the car pulled in front of her house, she stepped down off the porch to see Uncle Levy sitting in the driver's seat, grinning at her.

"Where you been all day?" Aunt Luella blurted out, before Uncle Levy could come to a full stop.

"Baby, Baby," he started.

"No, I don't wanna hear it," Aunt Luella said, turning her back and storming up the porch steps like a petulant child.

Since she was upset with Uncle Levy, we knew she wouldn't say anything to us, so we ran to the car and begged Uncle Levy to let us get in the back seat. He held the door open for us to climb inside and slither across the leather seats, my brother and I pretending we were racecar drivers barreling around the Nascar racetrack at dizzying speeds.

"C'mon, Baby," Uncle Levy pleaded, following Aunt Luella onto the porch.

He gave her a firm hug and a kiss on the neck, which seemed to soften Aunt Luella's rigid posture. He let his hands roam over her body, and when he eased them over her breasts, she slapped them away, looking around at us, slightly embarrassed by his open display of affection.

"Levy, you see dem kids over there," she said quickly.

"They seen breasts before," Uncle Levy replied jokingly.

"You such a fool," she said amorously, turning to give him a long kiss on the mouth.

"Um, now that's more like it," he said grateful for the change in her attitude.

"I'm still mad at you," she said, not letting him off the hook.

"What else is new?" he said teasingly.

Aunt Luella popped him with her hand across his stomach and sat down on the metal slider chair, Uncle Levy following.

"What we got planned for the evening?" she asked excitedly, but as soon as she saw the look on his face, the excitement turned once again to anger. "I knew it! I knew it! I don't know why I keep puttin' up with you!"

She stood up to go inside, but Uncle Levy stopped her, saying in a serious tone, "I got some business to tend to."

Aunt Luella paused, sensing in his voice that the business he was talking about could lead to nothing good.

"What is it now?" she asked sarcastically, knowing he could find trouble even if it wasn't looking for him.

"I can't get into it with you," he said, preparing himself to leave, knowing she would be upset with him.

"Go ahead. Leave then! Like you always do," she said.

"Luella," he said, pulling at her arm.

"Leave me alone!" she shouted, going into the house and slamming the door behind her.

We knew that was our cue to end our pursuit around the racetrack. We got out of the car reluctantly and hugged Uncle Levy.

"Tell your aunt I'll be back for me, alright?" he said getting into his Cadillac.

"Okay," we mumbled, returning to our dimly lit passageway, hearing the hum of the Cadillac heading down the dirt lane and turning onto Main Street.

A short while later we went inside the house to take naps, having tired ourselves from our active play. A couple of hours later, we woke and were put to work helping Aunt Luella prepare supper. We did it in silence as she was in no mood to talk to anyone. It was just getting dark good when we heard that hum again.

Excited, we started to run to the front of the house, but Aunt Luella growled at us, "Sit y'all asses down and finish those peas," and we slithered back to our posts, resuming our chores.

Aunt Luella walked to the front of the house and stood on the porch watching as the car headed towards her house. She stepped down off the porch, her face grimaced and her arms folded in irritation, waiting for the car to pull in front of her house. When it did, she saw Uncle Abe sitting in the driver's seat. He had just come from the Hatchet Joe's barbershop where Uncle Hank, Cousin Ned, and Uncle Levy hung out regularly, not necessarily to get haircuts but oftentimes to knock back a few shots of liquor and spend the day boasting and swanking, engaging in lively conversation about everything from running numbers to the Dollar Girl on the corner of Hines and Main Street to the Vietnam War.

Uncle Abe sat in the car saying nothing. We had made our way to the front door by then, thinking Uncle Levy was back, but when we saw Uncle Abe, he had a serious look on his face, and we could tell something was wrong.

"What's going on? Why you drivin' Levy's car?" Aunt Luella asked.

"I was down at Hatchet Joe's," Uncle Abe said, "and the sheriff came by."

"What'd he want? Is it Levy again?" Aunt Luella asked, thinking he had gotten himself into another altercation with another woman's husband. "Well, you tell that sumbabitch he can drop dead! I've been sittin' here all day waitin' on him to come by. And he go and get his ass in some kind of trouble. Then he be lookin' for me to bail him out. Not this time. No. Not this time, dammit. You tell him I ain't sittin' around waitin' on his sorry ass no mo'!"

"Luella...," Uncle Abe tried to interrupt her tirade but was unsuccessful. He got out of the car and followed her up onto the porch.

"I don't wanna hear it!" Aunt Luella shouted. "He got you to drop him off at that loose floozy, Velma's house, didn't he? And you did it too, huh? What kind of brother are you to stab me in the back like that? How could you do me like that? I thought you loved me!"

"Luella...," he started but was once again cut off.

"Naw, don't Luella me. What'd he promise you to keep quiet? Huh? Drive his car around to show off to dem bird-brained floozies down on Hines Street? He can buy you off that easy, brother? Really?"

"Luella" he tried once again.

"I can't believe you.   All y'all men are triflin', good-for-nothin', pain in the...," she stopped abruptly.

"Luella!" Uncle Abe shouted, grabbing her by the arms and startling her quiet. "Levy's dead."

With those words, Aunt Luella fell limp. Dead? Dead? The word rambled around in her head. She had never imagined Uncle Levy would ever leave her. As much trouble as he seemed to stay in, we all expected to one day hear he had been found dead somewhere, for not paying his gambling debts, but not Aunt Luella.   Somewhere in the back of her mind she always felt he would live forever.

"What happened?" she asked wearily, Uncle Abe helping her to the metal porch glider. "He owed some goons some money, didn't he?"

Uncle Abe paused. From the way Uncle Levy had lived his life, that would have been his likely fate.

"He didn't want you to know nothin' 'bout this." he began.

"About what?" she asked nervously, thinking it was dealing with Velma or some other woman.

"Hatchet Joe's barbershop got torched the other night," he continued. "The fire won't bad, but it did cause a lot of damage."

"What that got to do with Levy?" she asked.

"You know how Levy is. That quick temper of his. Hatchet Joe was like a papa to him," he said.

"And...?" she urged him on.

"Well, Hatchet Joe found out who was respons'ble. The sheriff told him he had been targeted," he noted.

"By who?" she asked.

"The klan," he replied in a serious tone.

"The klan? Hatchet Joe?" she pondered.

"Yeah," he said.

"Why him?" she asked. "For what?"

"For holding that voter registration drive at his shop this week," he said.

"You still ain't told me what that got to do with Levy," she said.

"Well, Levy wanted to pay 'em back. You know Levy. Don't mess with his family," he added.

"Why y'all let him get all mixed up in that?" she asked, starting to tear up.

"Like we could stop him once he got a notion in his head. He was determined to get 'em back, with or without us," he answered. "We tried to talk him out of it; even Hatchet Joe said let it go. He told him he would rebuild, but Levy won't havin' it. He decided he was gonna handle it himself, so he and June Bug ran up on dem klan boys leaving a honky tonk out on 301 Highway. June Bug's crazier than Levy is, will shoot you just as soon as look at you. June Bug said he got off a shot at 'em. But before Levy could get off a shot, one of dem klan boys hit him.

They got away, but Levy was hurt bad. June Bug drove him to Hatchet Joe's. But there was nothin' we could for him. He was too far gone."

Aunt Luella burst into tears upon hearing this news. Then she turned to Uncle Abe and lit into him with a fury, beating him in the chest, flailing her arms like a wild woman, angry at Levy, but because he wasn't there to receive the brunt of her anger, she wielded it at Uncle Abe.

"Why didn't y'all stop him! Why did y'all let him do that! You knew it won't gonna lead to nothin' good. Why didn't y'all stop him?" she cried out, Uncle Abe allowing himself to be a punching bag, and when she tired herself out, she fell into his arms and sobbed incessantly.

Uncle Abe helped Aunt Luella inside and had the painful duty of telling Grandma. An hour later Mama and Papa returned from church and stopped by Aunt Luella's house to pick up my brother and me. We were sitting on the porch crying in Aunt Luella's pine green metal glider when they drove up, parking behind Uncle Levy's convertible. They got out of the car, Papa carrying my sleeping baby sister, and walked up the porch steps. They were stunned to see us sobbing like that, thinking Aunt Luella had done something to us.

We were so distraught we couldn't move or talk, and before Papa could ask what was wrong with us, Uncle Abe came to the door and told them the news.

THE TOLL OF HIS WAR

Wearing his Marine uniform proudly and honorably, Henry Pritchard headed Stateside from the Vietnam War in March of 1970 to his hometown in Town Creek, North Carolina. There was no parade. There was no celebration. There was no family waiting for him.

He boarded the Greyhound bus in Camp Lejeune. The bus driver didn't want to cause problems, so he told him he'd have to sit at the back of the bus. As he made his way toward the back, he passed empty seats and seats filled with angry passengers who seemed to question, with their cold stares, his patriotism.

"How many women and children did you rape and kill over there?" their eyes seemed to inquire, Henry looking at them hoping to see some signs of appreciation for his risking his life for their freedoms.

As he passed one elderly white man, he felt the sting of spit hit the base of his neck, the moistness burning into his flesh like a branding iron. His pale face flushed a bright red.

"Sit down, Marine," the bus driver commanded, having watched the incident from the rear-view mirror and wanting not to cause any trouble on his route. "At the very back, Marine."

Henry advanced forward to his seat directly across from a Negro man of about thirty. The man watched Henry curiously, wondering what he was going to do to the old man, hoping he'd jump up and beat the shit out of him.

The Negro man thought to himself, "The most hateful thing you could do to a human being is to spit on him like a dog. Don't you agree, Soldier?" as if Henry could read his mind.

Henry just stared out the window of the bus as it made its way down the road toward Rocky Mount, North Carolina. The Negro man pulled out a handkerchief and passed it to Henry, tapping him lightly on the arm.

Henry looked at the man. This was the first act of kindness he had received since arriving back in the States. Then he looked down at the hand holding the handkerchief and noticed the Negro man had only one leg.

Henry's eyes asked, "How?"

The man mouthed, "The War."

Henry could hardly keep a tear from racing from his eyes. He took the handkerchief gratefully and turned back toward the window, wiping the spit from his neck, the loss of the man's leg reminding Henry of the toll of his War.

THE FEAR OF MY FATHER

My father was a Primitive Baptist preacher, and anyone who is familiar with the Primitive Baptist faith would know the word "Primitive" describes succinctly the doctrine of this denomination of faith. Primitive Baptists believe that we are all predestined to be "called" or "chosen" by God. Our names are already written on the Book of Life before we are even born, before we are even conceived as a being in God's mind.

"Many are called, and few are chosen," my father would always preach in his sermons. My father was a devout preacher. Elder Carper, he was called, after being ordained to preach the Word of God. My father read his Bible every day. I don't think I've ever seen him read another book, maybe the newspaper to see what the weather would be like for the week or to read the crop report, but other than that, he rarely read anything but the Bible. My father was a tall man, six feet, four inches tall and as thick as a running back for the local college football team. He liked sports, but only baseball kept his attention on Sunday afternoons after church. I think sometimes, maybe, he secretly dreamed of becoming a major league baseball player as much as he liked to watch it.

My father was a serious man, serious about business, his family, and especially the church. He believed that in everything he did, God should always come first. He prayed daily. It didn't matter where he was, if he felt the need to pray, he would. In the grocery store, at the tobacco market, on the tractor in the cornfield. We could hear him praying sometimes in the middle of the noonday, a scorching hot one hundred degrees, and he'd be singing the Lord's praises. As children, we wondered if he wasn't suffering from heatstroke or some sort of dehydration.

At night he'd always make us pray at our bedsides, on our knees, because kneeling showed your deference to God Almighty. We'd begin with a simple prayer that we children memorized before we knew our alphabets: "Now I lay me down to sleep. I pray the Lord my soul to keep. And if I die before I wake, I pray the Lord my soul to take." Then we could ask the Lord to answer any prayers we had been saving up all day. My prayer usually asked the Lord to bless my mother and father and sisters and brothers, except when my sisters or brothers angered me. Then I would pray something mean, but my father told me the Lord doesn't answer prayers made in spite, so I'd ask the Lord to forgive me and to bless my sisters and brothers anyway even though they made me mad. Then I'd end the prayer, "in Jesus's name, I pray. Amen." This would be our ritual every night that I can remember growing up in my father's house.

There were some days during my high school years where I'd skip my prayers at night, my thinking I was getting too old for that. Yet the fear of the Lord prompted me to remember and say an extra prayer whenever I'd miss one. My father would say, "You're never too grown for the Lord to whip you."

My father was a man that instilled fear in me, just from his voice alone. He only had to tell me once to do something or stop doing something, and I would. My siblings, however, seemed to test his every word. They failed. Their punishment? A belt whipping. A switching. Or a hand spanking. You'd think after a couple of hand spankings from my father, who had hands the size of a baseball mitt, they would learn to obey him on first call. But noooo. They were hard-headed, my father would tell them. "You need to act like your sister," he'd say, comparing my well-mannered behavior to their disobedient conduct. Only my obedience stemmed from my fear of him. I obeyed out of fear. The same fear I had of God.

My father fell ill when I was eighteen years old. Well, in actuality, he had a nervous breakdown. We never called it a nervous breakdown. We called it the episode. During that time, being anywhere near crazy was humiliating because, of course, you know people in small southern towns talked. Or better yet, gossiped. No one wanted their personal business to be the "talk of the town." There was such a thing as southern pride.

We failed to realize that our shame of his condition resulted in our denial of the seriousness of his illness. It was an illness and not an episode. If you think I feared my father before, I truly feared him after the episode. My fear was in the unknown. I had never known my father to ever lose control or to be so vulnerable as to want to take his own life as well as the lives of his children. I never thought of my father as weak. But that day I saw a weakness in my father, humanness, and I didn't know how to deal with that. I didn't understand it, so I could make neither heads nor tails of the situation. All I knew was my father had fallen, and I had no idea how to help him regain that stature that had made me fear him with the fear of God. I feared what he had become. What I couldn't know or understand.

MS. PIMMELLY'S CITY

I work in a city where magnificent older homes with verandas, high ceilings and huge sprawling lawns graced two-way streets lined with large beautiful oak trees; where maple trees blossomed every year with their colorful fall foliage; where old ladies sat on front porches in aprons, shelling butterbeans and black-eyed peas, peeling apples, pears, and peaches, and shucking corn; where young ladies scrubbed on washboards the day's wash and hung pristine white sheets cleansed in lye soap on metal wire strung from light pole to light pole and pinned with wooden clothespins to air out in the brisk country air; where children believed hanks hung low in the branches of trees late at night and waited to pounce on them at their least expected moment; where women worked hard in the cotton fields, tobacco fields, and on potato farms by day and gave birth to the next generation's future leaders by night; where hog-killings at the first frost were occasion for indulging in real pig slow-cooked over searing-hot coals for twenty-four hours, the flavor enhanced by oak and hickory hardwood; where the meat was moist and cooked thoroughly until falling off the bone, its succulent juices and smoky flavor creating a magical sensation on taste buds; where Eastern North Carolina-style barbecue and Western North Carolina-style barbecue both were as much a part of the regional heritage as they were cultural icons.

This was a city where Bible-verse spewing Jehovah Witnesses walked the neighborhood, casting their nets for souls; where young men smoked cigarettes rolled in paper; where old men chewed molasses-soaked tobacco leaves and spewed spittle from the corners of their mouths; where at one time the city was the hub of commerce, the seat of prosperity, a tobacco-processing town, which slowly divided itself between the east side and west side of the train tracks, with more people living without than with; where men thought hard, played often, and loved many in a town where slowly their livelihoods uprooted and moved overseas; where men settled arguments and disagreements with fists and foul language, or for the more reputable gentlemen of the day, duels, their choice of weapons, leaving one defending the death of the other.

Life was hard, real, meaningful. Families strived to stay together, creating familiar extended units that redefined nuclear families -- Grandma Esther, Great Aunt Ruth, and Jake, a second cousin once removed, all under one household.

This was a city where American Indians inhabited the region centuries before the migration of Europeans and Africans; where those Indians lived in the region now known as Wilson long before it became the city of beautiful trees; where life was the way it was supposed to be; where black people knew their place and stayed in it; where white people referenced black people as "Gal" or "Hey, you," and they answered, not out of a genuine sense of respect but out of a contrite existence fueled by buried anger and hatred which often masked a false sense of community; where klansmen marched in hooded sheets with police escorts, warning old blacks and young blacks to stay home or die; where old blacks wanted to just leave it be; where young blacks couldn't let it be and retaliated, deference and humility taking a backseat to black pride and civil unrest.

This was a city where wealthy whites came from old money, those die-hard Lincoln Towne Car owners, American-made only, their mantra. From the hands of the generations-old plantation owners to their descendents, they passed down the family-owned and operated businesses to the proprietors of new money, college-educated, Starbucks coffee-drinking, Saab-driving newbies, their money burning holes in their pockets.

136

The wealthy blacks ascended the social ladder slowly and infrequently, believing they had finally arrived because they were the few allowed to join the country club, the private school and the nondenominational church, and their admittance to these once-segregated institutions meant they had somehow collected on the generations-old debt to their black counterparts for the injustices enacted upon their ancestors, believing they were the restitution for years of slavery for other members of their race.

This was a city situated about twenty miles south of Gold Rock, the mid-point between New York and Florida, surrounded by nothing but farmland, beautiful maple trees and towering Long Leaf Pines. This was a city falling somewhere between the coastal plains and the piedmont, where the land was flat with gently rolling hills; where streams flowed through swampy lands; where tar and turpentine funded the economy of the early days; where cotton products eased in and tobacco slowly monopolized; where small towns with unique, colorful names - Tickbite, Lizard Lick, Rockfish, Frog Level and Frying Pan Landing - all welcomed visitors from the city to these neighboring towns. This was a city where hurricanes visited, disrupting the quiet serenity of the sleepy town, uprooting two-hundred-year-old trees and creating newly flooded waterways where there had been none before, where 500-year floods made untimely visits every 100 years.

This was a city the residents called home; where the local economy was supported by cotton pickers, tobacco processors, shirt pressers, pharmaceutical line workers, rubber mold operators and bindery workers; where surgical technicians, dialysis technicians, licensed practical nurses and registered nurses mended the sick and the lame; where volunteer firefighters and basic law enforcement officers risked life and limb each time they answered a call of rescue; where Liberty Bonds supported the war effort; where welfare benefits became the choice of payment for overdue utility bills, cable service and local extended phone service; where the unemployed grew weary and resorted to alternate means of financial support; where local law enforcement often turned a blind eye as long as the traffic never crossed west of the tracks that divided the haves from the have nots.

This was a city that became a haven for the mélange of new transplants invited to the sanctuary of suburban life, their migrant camps outfitted with only the basic necessities for sustenance; where educational opportunities and training were readily sought after by the steadily declining workforce; where outsourcing created a new class of people, the unemployed; where people like me attempted to re-educate the souls of this newly created class, laid-off workers whose jobs left them without a pension or retirement plan after thirty plus years of service, single moms forced to return to college to get training or a degree in order to receive child care benefits, no longer allowed to sit home and make babies, take care of babies, and receive a check, young people graduating high school seeking apprentice jobs that fifty-year-old men had forged the existence of and molded from the moment of inception, divorced housewives forced to provide for their families after their husbands of twenty years got the seven-year itch and no longer wanted the responsibility of being the sole breadwinner, and military retirees returning to school for training in a field that was non-combative.

I grew up in this town. Well, rather in one of the townships of Wilson. Elm City. I know these people. I understand these people. They are me.

Who am I? I am Ms. Pimmelly. A teacher to these people.

Book Club Questions

1. The stories in *Trouble Down South and Other Stories* are written from a number of different points of view. How do you think the points of view affect the stories being told?
2. What stories in *Trouble Down South and Other Stories* do you find the most interesting or compelling to read?
3. The story "Revolt in the Cherokee Nation" is written in prose form. What impact does this form have on the story?
4. In "Bastard Slave," how would you react to the story if it were not set during the "Cowboy Era"?
5. *Trouble Down South and Other Stories* contains a diverse set of characters in very different situations. Are there any common themes that recur throughout the collection?
6. In the stories, do any of the characters share overarching similarities?
7. How do the characters in these stories handle their "trouble down south"?
8. How do the characters in these stories deal with racism and slavery?
9. How do the characters in these stories deal with their feelings of anger and insecurity?
10. Several of the stories deal with a number of emotionally charged issues including domestic abuse, Post-Traumatic Stress Disorder, and mental illness. Do these stories provide a realistic portrayal of these issues?

CONTACT KATRINA PARKER WILLIAMS

Amazon Book Page

(I WOULD GREATLY APPRECIATE IF YOU WOULD LEAVE A REVIEW ON MY AMAZON AUTHOR PAGE) -- http://www.amazon.com/-/e/B004SR1OZK

Blog

http://troubledownsouth.wordpress.com/

Facebook

http://www.facebook.com/update_security_info.php?wizard=1#!/katrina parkerwilliams

Email

stepartdesigns@hotmail.com

OTHER WORKS BY KATRINA PARKER WILLIAMS

Liquor House Music, the first novel written by Katrina Parker Williams, is a raw, gritty tale of a proud, yet bitter black woman, Laura Dunn, and her struggle to survive in an abusive relationship. Each chapter in the novel reveals, through flashbacks, aspects of Laura's troubled life as an abused wife and mother of three children.

"**Remembering His Voice**" — Published in *Patchwork Path: Treasure Box anthology*